Witches and Waterways

A WATER WITCH MYSTERY
BOOK THREE

LEAH R CUTTER

KNOTTED ROAD PRESS

Reviews

It's true. Reviews help me sell more books. If you've enjoyed this story, please consider leaving a review of it on your favorite site.

Come someplace new...

Are you a traveler? Do you enjoy exploring strange new worlds, new cultures, new people?

Sign up for my newsletter and I'll start you on your travels with a free copy of my book, *The Island Sampler*.

http://www.LeahCutter.com/newsletter/

Buy More!

Did you know that you can buy directly from the Knotted Road Press website?

https://www.knottedroadpress.com/shop/

Also by Leah R Cutter

Mysteries

The Water Witch Mysteries

The Witch is Inn

To Scratch a Witch

Witches and Waterways

Grilled Sand and Witches

The Lake Hope Cozy Mysteries

The Purloined Letter Opener

The Tell Tale Heart Pin

The Halley Brown PI Mysteries

Dancer in Darkness

Trophy Hunters

Collections

The Alvin Goodfellow Case Files

The Rabbit Mysteries

The Shredded Veil Mysteries

Magazine

Mystery, Crime, and Mayhem

Chapter One

"Are you sure you didn't send this to me? Or arrange for it to be delivered?" AJ said on the phone to her younger sister Bea, while holding the latest Valentine's Day card she'd received in her hand.

Bea gave an exasperated snort. "Why would I go to such trouble?"

"I don't know," AJ said, putting the card on her kitchen table, along with the other half-dozen she'd received so far.

That day was Friday the seventh, and she'd received one Valentine every day since the start of February. They were kids Valentine's Day cards, with cartoon characters saying corny things, such as a bee with a honey-dripping heart that said, "Bee Mine?", or a bear with an overflowing bucket of strawberries that said, "I can't berry to be without you!"

None of them were signed. They didn't come through the mail, either. Someone wedged them into the edge of her front door, as there wasn't a gap under the door. Sometimes they'd been soaked with the rain.

They didn't seem ominous or threatening. Just weird.

Okay, maybe a little creepy. But that was just because they were anonymous. The cards themselves weren't suggestive in the least.

"Maybe you did it because you thought I'd be lonely, or something," AJ continued. She looked out the kitchen windows into her back yard. The day had been gray and blustery. Night had already fallen and the rain would start slashing down soon. She hadn't gone into her yard and practiced her water magic in the fountain for a while—the weather had just been yucky.

She had had many opportunities to practice making water flow away from her, magically drying herself off after being caught in a deluge. Or three.

"Don't you have a date with Roland on Valentine's Day?" Bea said.

"Yeah," AJ said. Roland was the unofficial historian of Milltown. Since that wasn't a paying position, he had his own lawn and garden care business. Winters were his "off" season, so he'd had a lot of time on his hands to do research, write papers, and work for the historical society.

AJ and Roland been dancing around each other for a few months now. He'd lied to her soon after she'd first met him, and it had taken some time for her to trust him again. He'd been completely honest since then, and there had been a growing attraction between them.

They'd met for coffee or tea some afternoons, spent time talking about everything and nothing. It was finally time to see if there might be something else there.

Hence, dinner. Valentine's Day night. Roland had made reservations at one of the nicer restaurants the next town over, up the coast.

"Since you're already set up for the big event, why would I need to take pity on you?" Bea said. Though AJ considered herself the practical sister, and Bea was merely an artist, Bea still had a good point.

It was AJ's turn to sigh. "Because you're my bratty younger sister and would like to play a trick on me?"

"Fair enough," Bea said. "But again, I wouldn't do something as elaborate as this. Do you think Roland's behind it?"

"Ugh. I hope not," AJ said fervently. "'Cause if he is, we're not really suited for each other." Seriously, the thought of Roland being behind the cards was so off-putting to her.

"Have you asked him?" Bea asked pointedly. "You know, used your words like an adult?"

AJ rolled her eyes. "I will ask him," she promised. "I just wanted to ask you first."

"All right, I'll give you that. Of course, you'd think I was that brilliant," Bea said, sounding smug.

AJ fought back the urge to smack her sister, even though she was miles away.

"But you have no clue who it is? No vision to show you the culprit?" Bea continued.

"No," AJ said.

"Did you actually try having a vision about it?" Bea said determinedly.

"I did. Kind of." AJ picked up her soothing peppermint tea and headed back into the rest of her house. She thought of the kitchen and upstairs as the "private" areas of her house, the ones that were truly hers. The front entranceway, the round tower, and the large sitting room where she did her tarot card readings were the public places, those sections she shared with her clients.

Normally in the evening, she'd finish eating dinner, make her tea, then head upstairs to either the study or her bedroom. Tonight, she decided to go to her reading room and see if maybe she could get another vision.

She didn't feel the urge to go and sit in front of her scrying bowl. But she wasn't repulsed by the idea either. So maybe something would happen.

"It's probably good that you aren't having a vision about the cards you're receiving, though, right? Means they aren't dangerous?" Bea said.

"There is that," AJ said. Most of the visions she'd had so far had been about bad things that were going to occur. "Though you do know that mostly I see the future, not the past."

"So ask about who is giving you tomorrow's card, then," Bea said.

"That's a good idea," AJ said.

"See? I do have them, now and again."

AJ couldn't help but roll her eyes, even though Bea couldn't see her. "Do you and Peter have plans for Valentine's Day?"

"You don't want to know," Bea teased.

"You're right. There isn't enough brain bleach in the world for that kind of thing," AJ said, shuddering. She didn't need to think about her little sister and her adoring husband or any of the kinks they may have.

Bea just laughed. "And while I want all the details of your date with Roland, I don't want *all* of them."

"Deal," AJ said. Though she doubted anything *like that* would be happening. It was much too soon.

Even though she had been thinking about how soft Roland's beard looked, and how it might feel against her skin...

"You do know that if you were going to be alone and miserable, Peter and I would make a trip down to see you, right?"

"I know. Thank you," AJ said. Though she'd never been that close to her sister while they'd been growing up, they'd spent much of the past summer together, sharing the vacation house that Bea owned, and had figured out how to be friends.

"Mom's been making noise about coming down with me some weekend," Bea warned.

"She's made the same sorts of comments to me. I'll believe it after she's been here for an hour," AJ said. Their mother was urbane and sophisticated, and unlikely to be impressed with the sleepy little coastal town of Milltown, where AJ now lived.

It wasn't the town that kept AJ there, though she'd made more friends over the past nine months than all her years living in Seattle.

It was the ocean.

All she had to do was walk out her front door and she was on the beach. She could lose herself for hours sitting on the cold sand, being buffeted by the wind, smelling the salty air, watching the waves. She'd bought herself a wetsuit so she could go swimming. Since she'd come into her magic— an actual gift of menopause—she was unafraid of the strength of the waves or the undertow. She was still careful, but being fully submersed in water whenever she wanted to would keep her there in Milltown for a long, *long* time.

"How's the inn?" Bea asked.

"Payne is planning a big Valentine's dinner," AJ said as she pulled open the sliding barn door to her reading room. "We've had a couple of go-rounds about the menu."

Payne Thomas was the cook and general handyman at the Bridgewater Inn, where AJ still worked as a manager three-quarter time. He was a dedicated vegan, the most beautiful man AJ had ever seen, and he still gave her the willies when he started fervently talking about food.

He just had crazy eyes. Possibly from his time in jail, after his conviction for involuntary manslaughter and illegal drug use.

Unfortunately, despite cooking for years now, Payne just didn't have a good palate, or the ability to develop meals that the average person would like.

"Good luck with that," Bea said. "I'm surprised that you were able to get out of eating there with Roland."

"I claimed that Roland had already made the reservations and I couldn't back out," AJ said. Though in fact, she and Roland had only been talking about it, and no reservations had been made at that point.

AJ sat down at the beautiful carved oak table that the original owner of the house had left behind. On one side sat AJ's scrying bowl, a large glass bowl with swirls of blue and green spiraling up the sides. A collection of beautiful agates sat on a white dish beside the bowl, things she could use to disrupt a vision. For Christmas, Bea had given her a graceful pitcher from carved glass, that AJ kept filled with water for her visions. Though she didn't consciously clean or change the water, it was always fresh.

A whitish ball made of selenite crystal, about the size of two fists, sat on the other side of the table. Willow, a person who worked at the inn and who fancied herself a witch despite her lack of actual power, had recommended AJ get it to help cleanse her spiritual space.

AJ had never had any sense that the ball was magical or did anything. Still, her clients appreciated it, and it added to the general ambiance of the room, which for the most part, was soothingly modern, with blue-green painted walls, white sea-shell sconces, and the large window overlooking the ocean.

"So how's your competition?" Bea asked next.

"She's *not* my competition," AJ said sharply. "She isn't even a psychic."

At the start of the year, a young woman named Carla Lowenstein had moved to Milltown and set herself up as a psychic. She had a shop right on Main Street, on the second floor of the McAuley building, above the saltwater taffy and sweets shop.

AJ had reached out a friendly hand, attending Carla's opening weekend, offering to put some of Carla's cards in the entranceway of her business if Carla would do the same for her.

Despite her old-fashioned sounding name, Carla was quite young, not even twenty-five. She was tall and blonde, with beautiful blue eyes that never lost their calculating edge and a smile that always had a bite to it.

Carla had agreed, but another client of AJ's had reported that not only had Carla made fun of AJ seeking to "help," she'd watched Carla throw the cards in the trash. After that, Carla had gone out of her way to make life unpleasant for AJ, calling her a fake and trying to steal her clients. She made snide comments about "other psychics" on the Milltown app—a discussion forum set up just for locals.

AJ wasn't worried. Though she had yet to develop Ursula's sense of who had magic and who didn't, she honestly didn't think Carla was special in any way.

Carla *was* a better con artist than most, and so had managed to draw in some people, even though it was still the off-season.

Come summer, AJ might have a worry, as Carla had a better location than AJ did to draw in tourists. For now, AJ had decided not to let it bother her.

"Have you heard about Carla's ghost box?" Bea said, being bratty. "Old Agnes swears that it let her talk with her grandmother."

AJ snorted with derision, though she did have a momentary stab of worry, as Agnes was one of her own most faithful clients.

"It's a fake," AJ declared. As far as she could tell, and Ursula, her mentor, confirmed, most ghosts passed out of the present and went someplace else. Only when they had unresolved trauma did they stay on.

Like Gladys, the ghost who haunted the Bridgewater Inn. Though AJ had finally had a vision and had been able to tell Gladys how she'd been killed, the ghost had stayed on, still demanding attention from AJ and everyone else, like a needy cat.

However, AJ felt as though the ghost's presence had

grown less strong. When she visited AJ, the temperature in the office barely dropped. Would Gladys move on one of these days? AJ wasn't sure.

In the meanwhile, everyone at the inn still made sure that no loose papers were stacked in the lobby or Gladys would scatter them everywhere.

"Are you sure her ghost box isn't real? That it isn't her way of connecting to the spirit world, like you use your scrying bowl?" Bea asked.

"Pretty sure," AJ said. "You've met Carla. Does she seem to be on the up-and-up to you?"

"All right. She is a little shifty. She's also young. And very pretty," Bea teased.

"Being pretty and young doesn't make you more talented," AJ said dryly. Sure, she was older now, forty-two and already peri- if not post-menopausal. She was still mostly skinny (old-woman menopausal-belly be damned), had more than just a few gray flecks in her dark brown hair, and age spots starting to dot the backs of her hands.

"Sure," Bea said, the sarcasm evident. "Uh-huh."

AJ shook her head but didn't rise to the bait. She might always be older than Bea, but that didn't make her ancient, no matter what her younger bratty sister implied on a regular basis.

After a moment's pause, AJ told Bea, "I'm going to see if I can manage a vision, to see if I can figure out who's sending me these Valentine's Day cards."

"Or you could wait until the fourteenth. They'll probably reveal themselves to you then," Bea pointed out.

"Yeah, no," AJ said. "Not patient enough for that."

"Okay. Text me if you learn something," Bea said. "Talk with you next week. Bye."

AJ swiped her phone off, then turned the sound all the way down. She didn't want to be disturbed if she did end up having a vision.

She looked around her peaceful room, enjoying the beauty of it, listening to the waves outside, the mostly quiet night. The rain had just started, a soft patter on the windows.

She didn't want to try to force herself to have a vision. Pushing her powers generally resulted in a Grade A migraine. However, she felt something of a fraud by not being able to figure who was sending her those cards.

"Okay. Here goes nothing," she said, reaching for the water pitcher and filling her scrying bowl. "Let's begin."

Chapter Two

The water in AJ's scrying bowl had a weird sheen to it, as though bright sunlight shone down on it.

That was strange. Normally, her waters looked cloudy, covered with wisps of fog.

Still, AJ practiced her deep breathing, count of two in and count of five out, calming her nervous system. She moved her head in circles and tried to relax all the muscles in her jaw, neck and shoulders, the places where she traditionally held most of her tension.

Then, AJ started her chant. "Who will leave me a Valentine's card tomorrow? Who? Who will it be?"

The words didn't come easily. She didn't find herself falling into a routine with them. They felt awkward, as if she wasn't asking the right question.

The waters stayed bright, looking as though they had nothing to hide.

This wasn't working.

Should she just empty her bowl and walk away?

The light was so strange, though. Was there a vision just

waiting to happen, even though she didn't feel the usual urge?

"Show me what you got," AJ finally switched to. "Show me. Show me. What you got? Show me."

Finally, her chant came easily to her, the words flowing. The color drained out of her bowl and the familiar gray smoke rose up, little clouds dancing and swirling on top of the water.

After a short while, the fog cleared away, leaving the water a silver color, like a mirror.

As AJ suspected, the vision had nothing to do with the cards that were being left on her door.

Instead, she saw an old-fashioned radio bobbing in the waves of the ocean. It was only a few feet out from the shore.

Was that her house in the background?

The radio floated along, the curved wooden top gently rising and falling. Instead of an abstract design, a carved flower took up most of the front, the petals outlined with pieces of wood. The material behind the flower was a dark green color. The needle on the tuning dial at the bottom of the radio fluctuated madly, going from one end of its range to the other. An antenna stuck up on one side of the radio, made from a brilliant green crystal.

AJ watched as the radio ran into trouble as it moved further from shore. The water rose up, hiding the dial, lapping at the base of the flower section. However, the radio couldn't turn around and make its way back to shore, though AJ had the sense that it wanted to.

Clouds raced across the sky, turning the day dark. The

waves grew rough. The radio struggled on, occasionally swamped by water, but the top of it still popping back up.

In the distance, AJ saw a rolling ball that crackled with lightning. It was maybe three feet in diameter, covered in menacing black and red spots. It would occasionally strike out, harmlessly hitting the water as it floated along about ten feet above the water.

It appeared to be on a collision course with the radio.

Lightning sizzled in the air. AJ could smell the burnt ozone. A chill passed through her.

The rolling ball struck to the sides of the radio, missing it a few times.

AJ gulped. She knew it was just a matter of time before the lightning actually hit the radio, setting it afire on the dark waters.

The force of the strike pushed the radio under the water.

It didn't bob up to the surface again.

AJ found herself automatically reaching for her rocks to break the surface of the water, ending the vision.

What in the world had that been about?

AJ leaned back in her chair, reaching for her peppermint tea and taking a large swig of it, even though it had now cooled.

In some ways, the vision was obvious. A person, as represented by the radio, was in trouble, and possibly going to die soon, probably by drowning. As the vision had been all symbols and not a face, it meant that the person's death was preventable.

But who was in trouble? And what did the lightning

represent? Was it just a natural phenomenon or did it, too, represent a person?

AJ didn't know anyone in the radio business. There was an electronics shop run by Jermaine, a few blocks off Main Street, in the southern part of town, near the abandoned sawmills that gave the town its name. However, he mainly fixed broken phone screens and retrieved data from dead hard drives. Did he even sell radios?

There wasn't a local radio station. But maybe there were some amateur radio operators in town.

However, AJ had the feeling that wasn't it. The radio wasn't necessarily a *radio*. It symbolized something or someone. Just as previously the vision she'd had with a skeleton shooting her—the skeleton had been the representation of someone, not an actual skeleton.

That led AJ back to her first question—who was going to die?

And was there a chance that this time, she might be able to prevent it?

Chapter Three

AJ dutifully texted Bea about her vision. However, Bea didn't have a clue who might be represented by the radio, though she'd been in Milltown for a lot longer than AJ and knew almost everyone. Besides Jermaine the owner of the electronics store, the only other person Bea could think of was maybe Fred, the local gossip.

Her thinking was that a radio spread news, so possibly Fred could be represented by a radio, as the unofficial news source for everything that happened in the town.

That didn't feel right to AJ, but she still agreed to talk with Fred the next day.

Frustrated with her lack of clarity, AJ went to bed early, only to be chased by ever darkening waves in her dreams.

She woke up feeling even more unsettled. Water was her element, and waves were her jam. It was very unusual for them to turn against her.

It was Saturday morning, and with a groan, AJ slapped off her alarm. She was tempted to call in sick to the inn, as it was the off-season and there weren't that many guests that weekend.

But then Sooli would worry, and possibly insist that someone deliver some of her famous *da ji ma*, or chicken soup, to AJ.

Not wanting to inconvenience anyone, AJ made herself get up, take a long hot shower and get ready for work. She only had to put in half a day at the inn, as she'd been slowly but steadily working her way out of a job there. Her goal was to be only part-time by the next off-season. She'd be able to spend more time on her psychic business by then.

Hopefully she'd have enough clients that she wouldn't feel the need for more hours at the inn.

That might not happen if Carla continued to work as a psychic as well, despite her lack of actual magic.

The day was cold and rainy, the wind whipping the drops around, the water seeking to get closer to AJ, as usual. If it had been warm and sunny, she wouldn't have minded. But she'd woken up unsettled, and the cold seemed to sink into her bones that morning.

That was one of the "joys" of being somewhere between peri- and post-menopause. She was always cold now. When she wasn't erupting with heat.

Her mom had assured her that it would only be a year or so of unpredictable changes and her internal thermometer being "broken." AJ had been suffering for eighteen months already, though. Hopefully her system would calm down soon.

Being a water witch hadn't helped that much with her symptoms, except her ability to wick away sweat so she didn't appear to be a sopping mess when she had a hot flash.

When AJ opened her front door, that day's Valentine's Day card slid from where it had been stuck and fluttered down to her feet.

AJ looked around but didn't see anyone lurking. Dang it! Who was leaving these? She reached back inside and left it on the entranceway table before firmly locking her door and heading out. She didn't need to read it now. She was certain it would be the same as all the others, something cartoony and corny.

As had become her habit that fall, AJ stopped at the Storm Brew Café on the way into work. Okay, so it was kind of out of the way, a few blocks down Main Street. As she wasn't helping out at the front desk that morning, she didn't feel too guilty about getting to the inn a bit later than usual.

The building that held the Storm Brew Café had originally been someone's home in the 1930s. It was still beautiful and Miguel, the owner, kept it in good shape. Like AJ's house, the front had a kind of tower built into one side, the wide windows fitted with window seats and plenty of cushions.

AJ saw Fred Hansen sitting in the window, madly scribbling in a notebook. Ever since that fall, he'd actually been writing regularly, not merely talking about it.

He might finish a book one of these days, heaven forbid.

Inside the café, just past the white-and-black checkered tile, a roped-off grand staircase led up to the second floor. AJ had been up there for meetings a couple of times—

Miguel had knocked down the walls between the bedrooms and created a large function space.

To the right of the door was a larger area that held the gas fireplace, tables, a couch, comfy chairs, and the few customers who were already there. To the left was a smaller room, with sturdy chairs, tables, and the counter for ordering.

Juli was working behind the counter, as overtly cheerful as always. AJ had never figured out her secret: good drugs, good sex, or was she just like that naturally? The barista had let her blonde hair grow out for the winter, with half of it falling down to one shoulder and the other half coming in layered, thick fuzz. Her eyebrow, nose, and lip were all pierced, and the full sleeve that covered her right arm was getting more filled in all the time.

"Good morning!" Juli called out to AJ as she walked up to the counter. "Do you want the special today?"

AJ considered. Sometimes she just handed Juli a five-dollar bill and told the barista, "Whatever." It delighted Juli to have someone to practice her wild concoctions on.

The problem was that only about three-fourths of the time were the drinks successful. AJ didn't mind being a guinea pig, but that day, she needed something more standard.

"What is the special?" AJ asked, considering.

"Raspberry chocolate truffle," Juli said. "It's for Valentine's Day."

That sounded a little too frou-frou for AJ that morning. "No, I think I'll take a regular chai this morning. With coconut milk, please."

"You got it!" Juli said. She paused for a second. "I'm

going to have to go get the coconut milk though. In the back. And I kinda need to stock up on a few other things as well."

"That's okay," AJ said. "I'll go say hello to Fred. Take your time."

"Thanks!" Juli said with a huge beaming smile.

AJ was never sure how Fred would greet her. He'd decided she was his muse. So instead of spending years writing The Great American Novel (yes, he always said it with all caps) he'd "practice" writing other things that weren't as important first, inspired by her.

Like murder mysteries featuring a small-town psychic and her sidekick, the debonair town gossip.

Only in Fred's mind could he be considered debonair. He was a thin man with a mopey brown mustache above permanently pouting lips. A fringe of dark brown hair clung to the bottom of his pale skull, while whisps still decorated the very top. AJ wasn't sure how old he was— maybe in his late forties. He was the nominal manager of one of the smaller grocery stores in town, though AJ had never actually seen him working. Dressed in comfortable flannels, jeans, and solid work boots, he looked much more rugged than he actually was.

Fred saw her approach and held up a finger on one hand while he continued scribbling for a moment, before he looked up and smiled at her.

"So good of you to visit me today, Lady Muse," he said, giving her a bow from his seat.

"It appears that you really don't need me today," AJ said.

"I'd never refuse a visit from you," Fred said. He

paused, looked around the café for a moment, then leaned forward. In a conspiring tone, he continued. "Particularly since I am almost finished with my book!"

"Really?" AJ said. She was shocked. Fred had been working on his first book—The Great American Novel—for *years*. Possibly decades. Yet, he'd managed to write a second one in only four months. "How did that happen?"

"I don't know!" Fred said. He sounded surprised at himself. "But the murder has been solved, the murderer has been taken away by the police, and the psychic and her amazing sidekick are talking about what they learned about the case. The ending is wrapping up quite satisfyingly."

"Wow," AJ said. "Congratulations! That's fantastic!"

"Yes," Fred said with a smile. Then he grew serious. "And no. After I finish this book, what am I going to write next?"

AJ saw her in. "I may have another mystery for you to solve," she said, letting her voice drop down to just above a whisper.

"Really? Tell me," Fred said eagerly.

Fred didn't know that AJ had visions or worked magic. Few in town did. Fred assumed that Gladys the ghost sent her visions, doing all the work, not AJ. Despite the fact that AJ now worked part-time as a psychic.

A new thought occurred to AJ as she considered what to tell Fred—since the people in Milltown didn't know that she was actually a witch, maybe they couldn't see any difference between her and Carla.

"Do you know of anyone who owns an old-fashioned radio?" AJ asked. She brought out her phone and showed him a picture of a 1930s replica. She hadn't been able to find any that looked identical to the one in her vision, but figured the replica was close enough.

Fred thought for a moment. "Lee's Antiquities might have something like that in inventory, though I doubt it. That isn't Caitlin's style. Treasures by the Shore is going to be a more likely bet, as Sally's inventory is more kitschy. Why do you ask?"

"Gladys sent me another vision," AJ lied. It was easier for Fred to keep believing that.

"Ohhh. Is this someone who's in trouble? Or someone who is causing trouble?" he asked gleefully.

"In trouble, I think," AJ said, hedging her bets.

As the radio was a symbol, that meant that the person the radio represented didn't necessarily have to die. Particularly given how the radio had initially appeared to be happily bobbing along on the waves.

"The radio is a representation of someone," she added while Fred thought for a moment.

"I see," Fred said. "A symbol. Who in town could be represented by a radio?"

"Jermaine?" AJ guessed. "He does own the fix-it shop."

Fred shook his head. "No, too obvious. Besides, he deals with modern electronics, and the picture you showed me is an antique."

AJ nodded. She paused, then said, "You, maybe? A radio broadcasts news. And everyone knows that you're the person to go to if they want to find out what's happening in town."

Fred looked shocked for a moment, but then nodded. "I see where you're going with this. Ohh!" he said suddenly.

"What? What is it?" AJ said. Had he thought of someone?

"That's how the next book starts! You've just brought me my next novel idea! Thank you!"

Fred grabbed one of his notebooks and started scribbling madly.

AJ sat, ignored and a little miffed. She'd wanted some help this morning, not merely to act as Fred's muse.

Juli came up just then, carrying AJ's drink. "Here you go!" she said cheerfully.

"Thank you," AJ said automatically. She looked at Fred, but he was completely absorbed with whatever idea he'd just had.

"I'll see you later, Fred," AJ said, standing up, then pausing for a moment.

Fred waved at her with his other hand without ever looking up from the page.

AJ rolled her eyes at him, then walked out of the café. The weather hadn't gotten any better.

Neither had her mood.

Somehow, she just didn't think that Fred was the intended victim. Unless she killed him herself.

Plus, now that he had a new idea for a novel, he was likely to be scarce, not haunting coffee shops as he used to.

AJ hurried to the inn, all the while feeling put upon.

Fred wasn't going to be any help figuring out who was in trouble. Bea, though she was AJ's bratty younger sister, wasn't there either.

Nope. AJ was just going to have to figure this out on her own.

Whether she wanted to or not.

Chapter Four

After the lunch rush, the inn settled down enough that AJ didn't feel bad about leaving for the rest of the day. She was only supposed to work a partial day on Saturdays anyway. Generally, she had psychic readings to do Saturday evenings. However, two of her regulars had canceled, so AJ had canceled the third, determined not to feel guilty about having an entire night off.

She waved at Pedro sitting at reception as she left. He was one of Rosita's numerous cousins and often came in on the weekends to sit a few shifts. Particularly in the off-season as he was painfully shy and didn't actually like dealing with people that much.

Pedro was in his early twenties and very good-looking, with straight black hair, soft brown eyes, and a killer smile that he didn't use often enough. AJ had been coaching him, still searching for the right words to help him figure out how to make it a game for himself, so that he could be better at customer service.

The rain had at least paused temporarily, so AJ

wouldn't be soaked the moment she stepped out of the building. That didn't mean it wouldn't start up again sooner rather than later, as clouds still filled the sky.

Chances were, it would be a couple more months before she'd see sunshine on even an irregular basis. She was used to that from her years in Seattle. It was significantly more windy here in Milltown, but she'd grown to enjoy the howling she regularly heard outside of her window at night.

The front yard of the inn still had a lot of green, between the evergreens and the brilliant grass. The roses wouldn't wake until spring, and there weren't any flowers yet. However, there were already buds on the maples, and the crocuses had poked their heads out of the ground.

The inn took up the northern end of Main Street. Instead of walking home, AJ continued down the street. She headed toward Treasures by the Shore, figuring that Sally, the owner, might be able to talk with her about old-fashioned radios, or at least replicas.

Maybe someone had bought one recently? AJ didn't know, didn't feel as though she had much to go on at this point, but it could be a start.

Fred was no longer in the window when she passed the Storm Brew Café. He'd probably gone somewhere to write up his new idea.

She couldn't help but roll her eyes as she considered being a muse.

Well, she supposed she'd been called weirder things when she'd worked in the tech industry as a product manager. Her developers had spoken their own language it had seemed at times, and she'd had to ask them to explain things more than once.

Most of the shops she passed had some sort of Valentine's Day display in their windows—hearts, cupids, and red roses.

The salted-taffy and sweets shop had all sorts of chocolate and red candy on display in their window, along with some posters. The building was one of the more modern ones, with beige siding and a flat window. To the right of the window was a single door, which AJ knew from experience led to a small hallway and stairs, with doors leading to the various businesses in the building.

AJ slowed down as she approached the door, intending to look at all the posters. Mainly, she wanted to see if her *competition* was offering any sort of special séance for Valentine's Day.

Most of the posters were familiar to AJ, as she had many of them at the front of the inn. She'd even put a few in the front hallway of her house, including a "lovers" blood drive, an upcoming performance by a jazz trio, and a Valentine's Social that the local ice cream shop was organizing. It appeared that the saltwater taffy shop was also going to be participating in the social.

There was one poster hanging there that AJ wasn't familiar with. As she drew closer, she couldn't help but gasp.

An old-fashioned radio was displayed in the middle of the poster. It took her a few moments to process the words around it. (Seriously, someone needed to make better font and color choices: black letters in that curly font on brown wasn't very readable.)

It seemed that Carla *was* offering a Valentine's Day special. "Get in touch with your loved ones who've passed."

The radio was a representation of Carla's ghost box.

Well, crap.

AJ took a picture of the poster and texted it to Bea without comment.

Bea texted back right away.

So its your rival

AJ couldn't help but roll her eyes at the misspelling. Her sister always dictated her texts, then never went back to correct anything. It had made for some hilarious misunderstandings over the years.

*It is. She's never going to believe me if
I warn her.*

It was a few moments before Bea replied.

*I know. But you are still going to
worn her, right?*

AJ sighed. She knew she had to. It still wasn't going to be fun.

Yeah, I am. Wish me luck.

Several emojis of a four-leaf clover were the reply.

AJ pulled open the door. A waft of overly sweet air enveloped her. Jeez, she was going to get a sugar-high just by being in here.

She walked determinedly up the stairs. Walls and ceiling

were painted beige, and the carpet was dark brown. Did the landlord consider it easier to clean? Or had he or she recently repainted? There weren't any marks on the walls, so it was a possibility.

The stairs weren't too steep. What did Carla do for her clients who couldn't walk up these? Was there an elevator someplace? Or did she make house calls?

The smell of cheap patchouli incense smothered the smell of the candy about halfway up the stairs. AJ shook her head, wrinkling her nose and resisting the urge to sneeze.

Did Carla burn the incense to get rid of the sugar smells? If so, AJ didn't consider it an improvement.

Carla had decorated the outside of her rooms more since the first time AJ had been there. Tacky purple-and-black material now covered the walls around the door. She stopped and took a closer look. The background of the material was purple, with black witches hats and spooky cats done as black cutouts.

Plastic chairs now lined the hallway, giving the appearance of a dentist's waiting room. Except that they all had matching pumpkin pillows on them. So maybe a waiting room at Halloween.

Did Carla regularly have that many clients? All waiting for her?

The poster for the upcoming Valentine's Day special was on the door, a bit enlarged. AJ studied it for a moment. She didn't see a green crystal antenna on the radio. Then again, the radio itself wasn't identical to the one she'd seen in her vision.

She knew she was procrastinating. She honestly wasn't looking forward to trying to warn Carla.

As a responsible psychic, though, AJ felt it was her duty.

After a few more moments gathering up her courage, AJ raised her hand and knocked.

"Come in!" came the reply immediately.

AJ shook her head, opened the door, and stepped into the lion's den.

Chapter Five

"Oh. It's you," Carla said when she saw it was AJ.

"Love what you've done with the place," AJ said, trying but not succeeding at keeping the sarcastic tone out of her voice.

It looked like a cheap Halloween store had thrown up all over the front room. AJ had remembered seeing a few things in the room before, like the string of lights that were all pumpkin heads that lined the far window, the orange and black tinsel hanging on the wall, along with the prominent skull sitting on the desk in the corner.

Now, the lights had been dimmed considerably and all she saw was junk: a plushy black cat with an arched back; strings of gold coins like what a belly dancer might wear, hanging from the wall; mad-eyed creatures staring at her from the corner; and stuffed ravens hanging from the ceiling.

It took AJ's eyes a moment to adjust, for her to make out the large old-fashioned radio sitting on a table behind Carla. While it wasn't identical to the one in her vision—

the front was more ordinary, not a carved flower—it did have a bright green crystal antenna attached to the side of it.

There was something about that radio, something that caught at AJ's attention. Was it because it was so similar to what she'd seen in her vision? Was it the antenna, which seemed so out of place with the rest of it? Or was it something else?

Carla glared at AJ as she took in the rest of the room.

"Why are you here?" Carla said angrily.

AJ looked at her rival. Carla stayed where she was, seated behind her desk. She wore her blonde hair up that day, braided and pinned so it looked like a crown. Dark eyeshadow colored her eyelids—an exaggeration of what should have been a "smoky eye." Bright red lipstick overemphasized her mouth, making her look like a predator.

Yet at the same time, Carla's orange-and-black dress was large and flowing, dwarfing the girl, making her appear smaller than she was.

The message seemed mixed to AJ—both brash as well as shy.

"I had a vision," AJ said, figuring she could start with that.

"Sure you did," Carla said, the eyeroll more implied than given.

AJ explained the vision, about the old-fashioned radio being lost out at sea, becoming swamped by deep waters before finally being drown after being struck by lightning.

For the briefest moment, AJ thought Carla looked curious about her vision. Maybe even open enough to ask a question about it.

Then the barriers slammed shut, as if Carla suddenly remembered where she was and who she was talking with.

"So you're threatening me," was her cool response.

"No! No! Not at all!" AJ said, horrified. "I would never do that."

"Right," Carla sneered. "You just told me a vision you had about me being drowned."

"No," AJ said. "I saw an old-fashioned radio being drowned. That radio may or may not represent you. As it's just a symbol, there's a chance that the vision won't come true."

"Interesting take on it," Carla said. "So if you talk in symbols, that means it's more iffy of a prognostication. I like it," she said. "But you don't fool me. You're out to get me. Aren't you?"

"Why would I be out to get you?" AJ said, bewildered. "I don't know you."

"Because I'm taking your clients and eating your lunch," Carla said airily.

AJ snorted. "As if. My clients know the real thing when they see it."

"Yeah, right," Carla said. She paused a moment. "Is that it? Is that all you got?"

AJ stiffened, the words echoing in her head, reminding her of the chant that she'd used the night before.

"I'm not threatening you," AJ assured Carla again. "I'm just warning you to be careful of being on the water. That's all."

She knew it was possible that Carla's death might not come from drowning. It might be, though. That was, if the old-fashioned radio represented Carla.

There was a slight chance that it might not.

The eyeroll that Carla gave her was impressive, and AJ had grown up with a younger sister who excelled at such responses.

"Right. You're just telling me not to hold the séance tonight as part of the coastal cruise," Carla said.

"You're holding a séance on a cruise?" AJ said, surprised.

That sounded like a really good opportunity as a psychic. Maybe she should consider offering her services to one of the local tour boats. It would mean spending time out on the water, which was her element. As well as potentially expanding her client base.

Huh.

"It's on all the posters," Carla said, waving to one that was displayed prominently behind her desk.

AJ shook her head. She hadn't read all the details about the séance because the font was so bad. "I didn't know you were doing a cruise," she said truthfully.

"Several of them," Carla said. "Something that if you'd had any desire to succeed, you would have already set up."

AJ shrugged. She'd inherited Ursula's business, so she hadn't gone looking for additional opportunities.

Something she was going to have to remedy.

"So here's my warning for you, then, if you want to take it that way," Carla said, standing. "Stay out of my way, as well as my business. We are not colleagues, friends, or even acquaintances. It's a dog-eat-dog world out there, and I'm a much meaner pooch than you'll ever be."

AJ felt her smile grow sharp and bitter. "I used to work

in software, little girl," she said softly. "The old boys' club. You got nothing I'm afraid of."

They stared at each other for a few moments, silent and icy, before AJ turned and walked out the door.

Her steps as she stomped down the stairs echoed the words repeated again and again in her head.

Bring it.

Chapter Six

Of course, the news Sunday morning on the Milltown app was all about how Carla Lowenstein had disappeared after the séance on the coastal cruise Saturday night, before the boat had reached shore.

AJ's heart ached. She'd warned the girl, had tried to tell her to stay away from the water. Maybe her death hadn't been as avoidable as AJ had thought.

They hadn't found her body, but the search was still on.

Seemed Carla's business manager, Seamus of Top Talents, Inc., had been on the cruise as well. He claimed that it had to have been foul play, that someone must have gotten to Carla while she was on the boat, thrown her overboard.

But who?

Seamus was also calling for AJ's head. Carla had told him about her "threats."

She could already hear Bea's comment about how no good deed ever goes unpunished.

It didn't surprise AJ when a knock came on her door just as she finished her tea.

"Good morning Officer Naomi, Officer Brendan," AJ said when she saw the pair of them standing there. "Won't you come in?"

Though AJ thought it was weird to invite cops into her home, she knew that Bea would fuss at her a lot (A LOT) if she didn't. Besides, the police here in Milltown bore no resemblance to the officers in the Seattle Police Department whatsoever.

"Thank you," Officer Naomi said as she walked in. She was tall—a little over AJ's five foot ten inches—though she wasn't slim. Instead, she was broad and all muscles. Her red hair was cut short in a very androgenous style. The usual reddish freckles sprinkled across her nose had faded with the winter.

"Thank you," Officer Brendan said as well, though he sounded as if he meant it and also shot her a grin.

AJ had met both of the officers in their unofficial capacity a few times, such as at the Christmas festival that the inn had hosted, and the New Year's Eve bash that one of the local bars had put on.

Naomi was somewhat reserved even in public, possibly even a little shy. Her girlfriend/partner Iris, on the other hand, was warm and outgoing. It was obvious that they were completely in love with each other.

Brendan, on the other hand, was a complete and utter goofball with a loud laugh and a love of life. He was always interested in whatever everyone was doing, asking loads of questions, listening and remembering. He seemed to genuinely care about people. His perfectly round head gave him an innocent look, along with dark brown eyes that always held a spark of mischief.

While the officers might be a little intimidating because they were the police, she also knew them as people. So she would invite them into her home with little fuss.

In addition, they knew her.

"Can I get you something to drink? Tea? I might be able to rustle up some coffee..." AJ said as she glanced back at her kitchen. Coffee beans had been on her grocery list and she tended to do her shopping on Sunday afternoons. She might have a few left, enough for one cup...

"No, we're fine," Officer Naomi said.

Officer Brendan sighed, as if he would have really liked something to drink, but had to follow his partner's lead.

"I suppose you've seen the news," Officer Naomi said, coming to the point faster than AJ would have imagined.

"Yeah, I did. Poor girl," AJ said.

"Why do you say that?" Officer Naomi said.

AJ pressed her lips together. Until they found the body, Carla would be considered among the living.

However, AJ knew, *knew*, that she'd drowned. They would never find her alive.

So AJ tried to play it dumb. "She drowned, didn't she?" She knew that was what some of the other people on the Milltown app had been claiming.

"We don't know that for certain," Officer Brendan said.

"Oh, okay," AJ said. "So how can I help? Have you come to see me in an official capacity? As a psychic?"

While Officer Naomi made a face at that, Officer Brendan looked intrigued.

"No, we have not," Officer Naomi said before Officer Brendan could ask AJ about it.

AJ nodded and continued to wait. She knew that it was always better to let the police ask the questions rather than volunteer anything. Or at least that was what the cop shows always said.

"We heard that you went to visit Carla yesterday," Officer Naomi said.

"That's right," AJ said, nodding and smiling.

"What did you talk about?" Officer Naomi finally asked.

AJ knew she couldn't lie, particularly not since Seamus, Carla's business manager, had already been accusing her of threats.

"I had a vision which may or may not have been about her," AJ said. She explained how she'd seen the old radio drowned.

Both officers looked confused by that.

"That's it?" Officer Naomi said after a few moments.

"Yes, that's it," AJ said. Though she wanted to defend herself, to say that she hadn't threatened Carla or anything else, she kept her mouth shut.

The two officers looked at each other, then back at AJ.

"Did you say anything else?" Officer Naomi said.

"No," AJ said, shaking her head.

"Did Carla believe you?" Officer Brendan asked.

"No," AJ said. Though the following silence was slightly uncomfortable, AJ held her ground.

"Did Carla accuse you of threatening her?" Officer Naomi finally asked.

"She did," AJ admitted. "But I wasn't. I only told her

about the vision. I was trying to warn her to stay away from the water. I wasn't threatening her."

The two officers looked at each other, then back at AJ, their faces a mask. She had no idea what they were thinking. It must not have been good, though.

"Where were you last night between the hours of six PM and midnight?" Officer Naomi asked.

AJ sighed. "I was here. Alone. Took the night off. So I didn't have any readings or any clients come in."

"Do you normally have clients on a Saturday night?" Officer Brendan said.

"I do," AJ said. "But as two of them had already canceled, I went ahead and canceled my third, so I could have an entire night off." She had to wonder if the two who'd canceled had gone on the séance cruise instead. She wouldn't ask them directly, but she knew it wouldn't be that difficult to find out, particularly since Carla had gone missing. Most of the people who'd been on the cruise were also on the Milltown app, and had been chatting about their experiences.

"So, no alibi," Officer Naomi said pointedly.

"That's correct, officer," AJ said. "Is there anything else?"

The two officers looked at each other, then back at AJ. "Do you have any plans to leave Milltown in the near future?" Officer Naomi asked.

"I do not," AJ said. She figured going to dinner up the coast didn't count.

"I would advise that you stay in town until this gets solved," Officer Naomi warned.

"I will," AJ said.

The officers left soon after that. AJ shut the door, then let her forehead drop on it. She wasn't actually going to pound her head against the wood, though she did consider it for a brief moment.

She hadn't killed Carla. However, she wasn't certain how much that was going to matter, at least to the police. Would other people in town believe her? Or was she going to have to prove it to them as well?

Though a part of her wanted to step aside, stay back, let the police handle this, AJ suspected that she was going to have to solve this mystery herself.

If for nothing else, to clear her name sooner rather than later.

Chapter Seven

AJ had just finished putting her groceries away Sunday afternoon when she heard another knock on her door.

She wasn't expecting any clients. Hopefully it wasn't the police, come back to arrest her. Maybe Roland had decided to stop by? Except that no, Roland was out of town that weekend, visiting friends up in Seattle. Had he come back early?

Maybe it was whoever was behind the cards she'd found stuck to her doorframe. The one that day had arrived while she'd been out shopping.

AJ walked over and opened the door, determined to remember this time to get some sort of peephole for it.

Bea stood there—the last person AJ had expected to see.

"What are you doing here?" AJ said as she ushered her little sister into the front entranceway of her house. The rain had started up again, and Bea was soaked through.

With a wave of her hand, AJ dispersed the water so Bea no longer looked like a bedraggled puppy, her blonde hair suddenly poofy and dry. She wore a cute teal-colored raincoat that had a somber pink lining. Under that was an off-white blouse with reddish-pink stripes made out of dots, jeans, and waterproof hiking shoes. She looked more practical than usual, but then again, it was raining.

Bea shivered as AJ finished her magic, then she gave AJ a smile and a huge hug, holding her close for a few moments. "Man, if you could only bottle that somehow…"

"It is convenient," AJ admitted, returning the hug, then letting go. It still weirded her out that she sometimes hugged her sister now, as their family wasn't necessarily tactile. "But again, what are you doing here?" she asked as she turned and walked toward the kitchen, automatically reaching for the teapot.

"I'm here to support my stubborn older sister, particularly after she's been accused of killing her rival," Bea said. She walked over and opened the refrigerator, making herself at home as she pulled out a packet of cheese and some butter, as well as grabbing the loaf of bread sitting on the counter.

"No one's accused me of murder," AJ said sharply, suddenly wondering if she should be reaching for the wine instead.

"You haven't been keeping up with the Milltown app," Bea said darkly.

AJ blinked. She'd read it that morning, but hadn't been paying any attention to it for the rest of the day.

"What are people saying?" AJ asked, torn between dread and curiosity.

"There's a lot of speculation that you and Carla must have had some sort of long-standing feud going on," Bea admitted. "Carla had never had anything good to say about you. People assume you must have been talking derogatorily about her as well, just not in public."

AJ shook her head, bewildered. "You know me. You know that I haven't really given Carla any thought."

"Have you seen a drop in your clientele?" Bea said.

AJ shrugged. "Maybe? I don't know. This is the first year I've had a psychic business. Yes, things slowed down at the start of the year. I figured that was part of the whole off-season thing. Not that I was losing clients. I still have my regulars," AJ added defensively.

"Good," Bea said. "We'll lead with that."

"Lead? What are you talking about?" AJ said, still bewildered and thrown off by the fact that her sister was there.

"We're going into town tomorrow afternoon and sitting in the front window of the Storm Brew Café," Bea said seriously. "The only way to kill these sorts of rumors is to be very present and available."

"I have to work tomorrow afternoon," AJ said. "It is Monday, you know." Her sister hadn't had a real job since she was a teenager, so really wasn't bound by something as mundane as the days of the week.

"Take the afternoon off," Bea said with a dismissive wave of her hand. "Or at least take a really long lunch break."

"Are you serious?" AJ said, incredulous.

"I am," Bea replied softly.

AJ stared at Bea for a moment. Her sister seemed much more somber than usual.

"All right then." AJ took the teapot off the stove and reached for a couple bottles of wine sitting on the rack instead. She turned and silently held up both a red and a white.

Bea pointed to the red with a grin. "Now you're talking."

"Fine," AJ said as she opened the bottle and poured them both a glass. She got out some of the rotisserie chicken that she'd been planning on eating that night and put that on the table with the bread and cheese. It was after four PM. Close enough to dinner.

"Don't you have any carrots or cucumbers or something? Maybe a salad to go with this?" Bea asked, getting up and walking back to the fridge.

"Yes, Mom," AJ said. "Bottom right."

"Pasta salad doesn't count," Bea said primly.

AJ couldn't help but roll her eyes. "There are carrots in the drawer. And a couple red bell peppers."

"Color!" Bea exclaimed as she pulled them out. "I thought you primarily ate a white diet. You know, all your food being beige and white?"

AJ held up her wine glass. "This isn't white," she pointed out. "Not only that, wine counts as a fruit."

Bea sighed and shook her head but didn't say anything else as she fixed them both a few vegetables to have with the rest of their meal.

"Milltown is a small town," Bea said slowly after she sat down again. "And it's the off-season, so people aren't busy. There's going to be a lot more gossip than usual. Plus, you're still new to town. Since people haven't known you forever, they're more likely to turn against you."

AJ nodded, considering. "But they know *you*," she said after a few moments.

Bea gave her a brilliant smile. "Exactly. They know me. They'll see us together, that we're still friends, that I'm supporting you. That will put an end to some of the worst of the gossip. Not all of it, but a good portion of it."

"I think Fred will be on my side as well. If he's around," AJ said. She told her sister about their latest conversation, how she'd "inspired" Fred's next novel.

"So Fred knew about the vision as well?" Bea asked.

"He did," AJ nodded. "If we can persuade him to put aside his latest book, he could even tell people that. That I didn't know exactly who was represented by the old-fashioned radio."

"That's good," Bea said. "We'll get this taken care of. You really, *really* don't want to ruin your reputation down here. Particularly not when you have a business to run. Two businesses, both the psychic thing and the inn."

"Why are you so adamant about this?" AJ asked.

"I've seen it happen," Bea said grimly. "Carolyn did jewelry. Pretty generic, but she had a good business, and a large online presence. She had a *very* public falling out with her spouse, Terry. They'd both had too much to drink and went to a New Year's Eve party at one of the bars on Main Street."

Bea took a deep breath as well as a big drink of her wine before continuing. "She accused him of some nasty things. The fight turned violent. Cops had to separate the two of them. Terry claimed later that those accusations were confessions, when he went public with 'proof' of Carolyn's affair. Even though everyone agreed that Terry had been the aggressor in their fight, the entire town ended up siding with him. Despite how later, Carolyn 'proved' that it really had been Terry having the affair. It was a mess."

"Sounds like it," AJ said. "What happened to Carolyn's business?"

"Even more rumors," Bea said, rolling her eyes. "You wouldn't believe the things people started saying about her, perfectly reasonable people. It was worse than those talk shows with all the conspiracy theories. She left town the next winter. I think she's still running her online business—it's kind of what saved her. Despite the A-holes giving her bad reviews on her site."

"What happened to Terry?" AJ had to ask.

"He also left soon after she did. People kind of turned on him as well. It was almost as bad as when Sheriff Cavallo was accused of election fraud."

That stirred a memory in AJ. "I remember Ursula talking about that," she said slowly.

When Bea motioned for AJ to continue, she told Bea how Ursula had had a vision of the sheriff giving his acceptance speech. It had been a vision without context. Ursula had had no idea what to do with the information, not until the sheriff was accused of buying votes.

Bea nodded slowly. "I remember how the tide rose against him, as even here, people don't always trust the government. But it turned, slowly. It's a good thing the sheriff is a likeable man."

AJ nodded. "And the case against me?" she finally asked.

"Seamus Miller is a problem, as he's the one who is currently the most vocal about you being guilty," Bea admitted. "You're never going to convince him of your innocence. Instead, you just need to keep the rest of the people on your side."

"Or else?" AJ asked.

"Or else that radio you saw? Sinking under the waves? That might be you."

Chapter Eight

Roland called AJ as she was walking to the inn Monday morning.

"Good morning!" he said cheerfully.

"Hey there," AJ said. She couldn't help the goofy grin that took over her face at the sound of his voice. Jeez. And they hadn't even gone on their first date yet.

"How are you holding up?" Roland asked seriously. "Is there anything I can get you? Can do for you?"

AJ laughed softly at his earnestness. "Find me Carla's killer?" she asked.

"I'll work on it," Roland promised her. "What happened between you and Carla? I know you hadn't even expressed interest in her, all the time I've known you."

That warmed AJ, that someone besides Bea had understood her stance about the other psychic. She explained that she'd had a vision, and had gone to warn the girl.

Roland accepted that AJ had visions without question. Then again, he also believed in ghosts, and continued to try to talk with Gladys. Unfortunately, the ghost didn't want anything to do with him. Plus, she didn't come to visit AJ as often as she once had.

AJ had yet to tell him about the magic, about being a water witch. One step at a time. She didn't feel as though she was lying to him, not exactly. Visions felt like a bigger part of who she was, rather than throwing water around.

"I figured you hadn't 'threatened' her, or whatever else they're claiming," Roland said. "But no one else knows you had a vision, right?"

"Just a few. Including the police, who visited me yesterday," AJ said.

"I know a couple of hot-shot lawyers, if you need help," Roland said seriously, meaning his parents, though she didn't think either of them had any experience in criminal cases such as this.

"Thanks," she said, still touched by the offer. Roland wasn't on the best of terms with his parents. That he'd offer their assistance meant a lot.

"Do you need some company?" Roland said. "I could swing by later if you need someone to talk with."

"Thank you, but Bea came down," AJ said.

"Oh, okay," Roland said. He paused, then asked quietly, "So are we still on for Friday?"

"We are," AJ said. "I rejected Bea's offer that we make it a double date." As Peter was coming down on Friday, they could have gone out together.

"Oh, thank you," Roland said fervently.

"What, don't want to face having to make small talk with Bea?" AJ asked, amused.

"No, I don't relish getting grilled by her and Peter, that's all," Roland said.

"Speaking of being grilled…"AJ said. "I have a question for you."

"Okay," Roland said. "I'm sitting down and I've put my coffee on the table, away from my book. I'm ready."

AJ snorted. "I've been getting Valentine's Day cards every day. They're little kids' cards. Are you sending them to me?"

"No," Roland said, sounding surprised. "Do I have any reason to be jealous? Is there somebody you're not telling me about?"

"No, absolutely not," AJ said, relieved. "I don't know who's sending them. And it's getting a little creepy."

"So I shouldn't send you anonymous Valentine's Day cards?" Roland said slowly.

"That's correct. And you wouldn't lie to me, right?" AJ said, clarifying.

"Never again," Roland said fervently. "It isn't me, though."

"I thought not," AJ said with a sigh. If it wasn't Roland, who was sending them?

The pair of them talked for a while about his trip to Seattle that weekend before AJ signed off as she walked through the front courtyard of the inn.

Though AJ and Roland might have started off rocky with him lying to her, things were certainly going better now.

Hopefully, things would continue to work out between them.

Sooli was working behind the reception desk. She gave AJ a big smile when she came in. "So good to see you!" she said pointedly.

AJ hadn't realized that she'd been worried about the reaction of the people at the inn. Sooli was obviously determined to let her know that she, at least, supported AJ.

"Thank you," AJ said, the relief flooding into her like a warm spring shower. "I'll be right back."

She hurried back to her office to put away her purse. The office was a cool sixty-three degrees when she arrived. That was the coldest it had been in quite some time.

"Good morning, Gladys," AJ said, greeting the ghost who haunted the inn. She'd hung a large thermometer in the office so she'd be able to keep track of the ghost's effects.

Surprisingly, a foggy figure appeared on the far side of AJ's desk. Gladys's features were never distinct: vaguely female shaped, floating several feet from the ground so she gave the impression of being much taller than she actually was.

AJ was impressed. Gladys must be using up all her energy if she not only froze the room but had also made herself appear.

Vision.

The word floated between them, the coldness in the office suddenly intensifying.

"What, you want to show me something?" AJ asked, surprised.

The last time Gladys had shown AJ a vision, it had been of her own death.

Did the ghost have some sort of connection to Carla that AJ hadn't realized?

AJ quickly beat down the surge of jealousy that rose up. Gladys wasn't just *her* ghost. Though AJ was still certain that Carla had been a fake, perhaps Gladys had still been drawn to her for some reason. Maybe her claims of being able to speak to ghosts had been of interest to Gladys.

Though how the ghost would have heard about it, AJ wasn't certain. Maybe there was a ghost network. Roland did claim that some of the ghosts he talked about on his famous ghost tour of Milltown were real.

AJ pulled her water bottle out of her purse and grabbed the bowl she kept on the corner of her desk just for these occasions. She'd been using a bowl that she'd taken from the kitchen, but after Payne had taken it back, she'd brought in a beautiful handblown glass bowl she'd seen in one of the shop windows at Christmas time. It was red and green with a swirl of white dancing through it.

After AJ poured the water into the bowl and sat, settling herself, the expected cold touch began. It started in the center of the back of her neck, then shot along the tops of her arms, as if they'd suddenly been doused with a freezing spray. She couldn't help but shiver as she gazed into the water.

The water had a strange sheen to it again, as it had before with the first vision about Carla.

What did that mean?

After just a few moments, though, the familiar wisps of fog sprang up. They only danced for a short while before the water cleared, turning into a silvery mirror-like surface.

Instead of a figure rising up, out of the mirror, AJ found herself flowing down, beneath the water. She quickly found herself in the waters of the ocean, just off the coast. She was familiar with the blue-green color, the cold that seeped in, even in her wet suit, the slight smell of salt water despite the mask she wore.

Down she went, moving faster than she could swimming, even with fins. The water still buoyed her up, and she relished how light and sleek she felt.

It was a different experience for her to be an active participant in a vision.

Finally, though, she got to where she was going.

AJ shivered, looking at the dead body of Carla.

It wasn't a real dead body, though. Carla looked exactly as she had the last time AJ had seen her, wearing that too-large dress that floated all around her, her blonde hair up in braids on top of her head like a crown, with too red lips and exaggerated dark eyes. She sat in full lotus position, just above the ocean floor.

AJ had the impression that Carla was more at peace, now, in death, than she had been living. She wasn't happy, she didn't have a beaming smile. But still, content.

Carla looked AJ up and down, clearly surprised. Abruptly, she nodded, then she lifted one arm and pointed up above her head.

AJ looked, but didn't see anything.

A whooshing noise filled AJ's ears. Suddenly, she shot toward the surface.

She momentarily feared getting cramps, changing pressure so abruptly, but no. Everything was fine.

She popped out of the water and continued going, until she found herself standing above the water, the waves tickling the bottoms of her feet.

Looking around, AJ recognized exactly where she was. Just off the edge of the coast, down to the south of Milltown, directly out from the point. She could just make out

Sandy's Grill, the restaurant that took up much of the coast there.

Dang it!

A splash in the water made her look down. It was all black beneath her.

When she looked up again, she was back in her office. She'd automatically plunked a black binder clip into the water bowl to break the vision.

AJ sat back, shivering with the cold after effects.

A question hung in the air—a layer of expectation flowing around her like the chill that was finally starting to recede.

Slowly, AJ nodded, though she could feel a headache edging in from the outskirts of her skull.

"I saw," she said slowly, her voice croaking. "I'll let... someone know."

Satisfied, Gladys withdrew. The temperature in the office quickly rose.

AJ found herself still shivering.

She had no doubts that Gladys had just shown AJ where Carla's body lay.

The ghost obviously expected AJ to help.

Why, AJ still wasn't certain. Or even how Gladys had known.

However, if AJ went to the police with the exact location of Carla's body, that was just going to incriminate her further.

What was she going to do?

Chapter Nine

AJ met Bea for lunch at the Storm Brew Café. She'd cleared taking a couple hours off with Sooli before she left the inn.

AJ ordered her favorite cheese, turkey, and tomatoes grilled panini, while Bea got a far too healthy salad. Then, it wasn't until after they'd gotten their food that AJ said anything about the vision.

"Don't tell anyone," were the first words out of Bea's mouth.

"Not helpful," AJ said. "I have the feeling I need to tell someone. Or I'm going to have a pissed off ghost at the inn." Despite the fact that Gladys hadn't been manifesting as much, AJ assumed that might be subject to change.

"Will Gladys cause that much trouble?" Bea asked.

AJ tilted her head from one side to the other. "For the most part, we've minimized the damage that Gladys can do. We don't keep any fliers in the lobby. Some idiot just dropped off a bunch one time, before Christmas, without asking anyone. Gladys shredded them like confetti. Even Rosita complained about trying to clean up the mess."

"So she can't do much?" Bea said.

"No, that isn't it. It's like the lobby is fair game, but Gladys never steps behind the reception desk. My fear is that boundary may disappear if we push her too far," AJ said. "And we do keep papers back there."

"That would be a problem if Gladys decided to target the reception desk," Bea agreed.

"Who can I tell this to, though? I need someone who can do something about the information," AJ said. "without totally incriminating myself."

"Fred, maybe?" Bea suggested. "He's always claiming to have anonymous sources and tips for the gossip he gathers."

"If we can find him, that's a good idea," AJ said. "And I think he'd be willing to keep my name out of it."

"I'm still not sure you should tell anyone," Bea warned.

AJ shook her head. "I have to. It isn't just the threat of Gladys misbehaving. It's like an obligation." She paused, taking a bite of her delicious sandwich, thinking. "Imagine how Mom would feel not knowing if you were dead or alive."

Bea smirked. "Mom would be threatening to kill me herself if I just disappeared."

"I'll give you that," AJ said, grinning. "Still, she'd be worried."

"I know," Bea said, sighing. "I just don't want to see you getting into trouble."

"That's why we're here, right?" AJ said brightly. "To put to rest those rumors? To see us presenting a solid front for everyone else?"

"That's right," Bea said. "Keep smiling and be willing to talk with everyone."

The sisters chatted as they finished their respective lunches, Bea going back to the counter to fetch them some coffee afterward. AJ had let Juli make her a "whatever." Bea had come back with a delightful mint chocolate concoction that made for the perfect dessert.

While they sat and talked, AJ saw a few people walk by the window and glance up at them. Mostly people looked neutral, but AJ caught a few grimaces thrown her direction.

Hopefully seeing that Bea was beside her would help change their minds about her.

Miguel, the owner of the café, came up to them before they'd finished their drinks. He wore a stained white T-shirt and a gray apron over his jeans. He didn't look like the owner, but rather, like everyone's favorite uncle who worked here as a dishwasher. He walked directly up to AJ and gave her a one-armed hug, silently showing his support.

Bea stood up and got a bigger embrace, partly because they knew each other better, but also because Bea was just a more tactile person than AJ ever would be.

"If I'd known you were coming in, your meal would have been on the house," Miguel told AJ seriously. "We support our friends. I'll let Juli know for next time."

"There's no need for that," AJ assured him, though his words touched her.

Miguel just grinned at her. "It's good business," he said. "Though I don't think the town will be that divided over you, those who support you will also come here, to show their support."

"So you'll get more business because you support me?" AJ said, bemused. "Not less?"

Miguel shrugged. "Customers come and go. There are

always upswings and down. I can always get another job if it comes to that."

AJ knew that the chances of him actually needing a second job were slim. The café continued to do well, at least according to the rumors she'd heard at the chamber of commerce meetings.

"Still, thank you," AJ said, touched.

Miguel talked with them for a bit, showing his support, before he retired back to the kitchen.

Just as AJ was considering going back to the inn, Fred came in. "I'll be right there," he told the sisters before he dashed to the other side of the café to order his own drink.

"Seems that Fred also wants to show his support," Bea said, amused.

It touched AJ that some people might come to her defense, even though she'd only been in Milltown for ten months or so.

Then again, she knew more people here, and felt as though she had more friends in Milltown, than after all her years in Seattle.

Fred came bustling back with a to-go cup, something that AJ had never seen him with the entire time she'd known him. He *always* sat and drank his coffee leisurely.

Then again, since he'd started writing seriously, he hadn't been in coffee shops as often.

Maybe he still supported them, came to get his coffee and to take a break, but then would go back to his own apartment (just up the hill on this side of town) to write.

"How are you, my dear muse?" Fred asked gently AJ as he pulled up a chair to sit near them.

"I'm doing fine," AJ said.

"Muse, huh?" Bea said with a sly grin.

"Not only has she inspired the first book I've just now finished, she's also given me the idea for the second!" Fred said, beaming.

"So I heard," Bea said. "But how can you keep up with everything going on in town if you're not here, in the thick of things?" she teased.

However, Fred answered her seriously. "I can't," he said. He sounded a little sad at that. "I used to know everything, *everything* going on in Milltown. As well as the two towns closest. Things happen now and they *surprise* me." He paused, then grinned. "That part's both a shock as well as kind of nice."

"I see," AJ said. She recalled being in an office managing a team of developers and knowing what was happening in all of their lives. Even the ones who didn't normally share anything personal still had talked with her.

It had been strange. Was it because she'd been one of the few female managers in the company? Because she'd actually cared and tried to listen? Or because she'd gone out to happy hour a few times when people had over-shared, and it had become a habit?

She'd actually been the closest to one of the remote people she'd managed. He'd managed her in return, always letting her know what he was working on and when he was running into difficulties. She sometimes felt she knew more about him than the people sitting just down the hallway from her, who also supposedly reported to her.

"But, I read some of the terrible things being said about you on the app!" Fred exclaimed. He nodded at Bea. "Very wise of you to come down, to support your sister. To be here as well."

AJ was glad that Fred got it.

"I'm really happy to see you, Fred," AJ said earnestly.

"Why? Do you have another story idea to infest me with?" Fred said, only partially joking.

"What? No," AJ said. "I do have something to tell you about. That I'm hoping you might be able to share with the right people."

"Oh!" Fred said quietly, furtively. "You had another vision!"

"Yes," AJ said, nodding. "Gladys gave me another vision." She was surprisingly glad that she wasn't lying about the source of her vision for once.

"What was it?" Fred asked, eager to get the scoop before anyone else.

AJ sighed. She looked at Bea who nodded her encouragement.

"Gladys showed me where the divers will find Carla's body," AJ said softly.

"Oh!" Fred said, followed by a more thoughtful, "oh."

"Yeah," AJ said as Fred reached the appropriate conclusion, figuring out just how much this would incriminate her.

"Huh," Fred said, sitting back in his chair and sipping from his to-go cup, thinking. It took him a few moments before he said, "Okay. I've got an idea how to spread this around. Tell me where to direct the divers to look."

With great relief, AJ told Fred, how they needed to go straight out from the southern point.

"Got it," Fred said.

"Thank you," AJ said gratefully.

Fred shrugged. "That's what friends are for. Plus, I still owe you for that fantastic idea for the next book. And this is just going to play into it nicely."

He stood abruptly. "All right. I have some rumors to plant and a novel to get back to. Those words aren't going to write themselves! See ya!"

He didn't quite take off at a run, but almost.

Bea looked perplexed at AJ. "I know you told me that he'd really started writing. I don't think I'd believed it until now."

AJ shrugged. She wouldn't have necessarily believed the change that had come over Fred either.

"Now, what?" AJ asked as Bea started getting ready to go.

"Now, we hope that your vision was accurate and that Fred's as good as his word."

AJ nodded. "See you for dinner?"

"Yup," Bea said. "Come by the house when you finish work."

"Will do," AJ said.

She walked back to the inn a bit more confident than she'd left.

Once the divers found the body, maybe there would be evidence of foul play, and AJ's name could be cleared.

Though somehow AJ knew it would never be as easy as that.

Chapter Ten

The text from Bea later that afternoon took AJ by surprise.

Milltown app. Go reed.

AJ just snorted at the misspelling but did as Bea had instructed. She'd been avoiding the app because she hadn't wanted to see what people had been saying about her.

While some of the people posted with their names, or even with the names of their businesses (like 2OldLadies, who ran an extremely successful animal sitting business, and who always posted the most adorable pictures of their personal pets) some people still posted anonymously. It was always a game, seeing if they'd leave enough information accidentally so that someone might figure out who they were.

A couple of new anonymous posters had joined the chatter since the last time AJ had looked at the app, or at least two names that she didn't recognize.

One was GrayDawn, who appeared to have known

Carla and was, like Seamus, accusing AJ of being behind her death. GrayDawn's account had been started after the first of the year, though there didn't appear to be that many posts from them until now.

AJ scrolled through a number of messages, just reading the first sentence or so of each for more than a page. About half the people were convinced that Carla was dead, while the others were certain that she was still alive and would be returning to town shortly.

Finally, AJ scrolled down to the most recent post, by yet another anonymous account, EarlyRiser. They announced that they'd seen something floating straight out from the point south of town, while they were eating at Sandy's Grill. Perhaps a body.

AJ snorted. Well, that was one way of getting the word out. She wasn't certain how Fred had set up the anonymous account. Then she went looking at the history of Early-Riser, who had actually created the account back in May the previous year. The person had only posted four times total in those ten months, all spectacular sunsets.

It was good that the information was out there. Hopefully, someone would notice it.

A second account, run by Pricilla Strong, the owner of the ice cream store close to the waters, claimed that she'd seen something too.

AJ knew that Pricilla hadn't. Carla's body was far beneath the water. Had Fred contacted her, and asked her to post something as well? AJ suspected that might be the case, as Pricilla would love the attention.

Then Sandy herself, from Sandy's Grill, claimed to have seen something.

From there, it snowballed. People started urging the searchers to move the area they were diving in down the coast. Instead of looking where the boat turned around, they needed to look closer to where it had docked.

It wasn't until Tuesday morning that the police finally confirmed that Carla's body had been found, right off the point, probably in the exact spot AJ had seen.

AJ's morning had started out fairly rocky, with spilled coffee when she'd tried to make some at home. Juli hadn't been behind the counter at the Storm Brew Café and Juan, her sub, had added too much coffee and not enough cream to AJ's order, making it bitter enough to turn her stomach. Then, Payne had been on a tear and AJ had had to act as mediator between him and Rosita.

As the day had started so badly, it didn't surprise AJ in the least when a quiet knock came on the office door midmorning, and Willow showed Officers Naomi and Brendan in.

"How can I help you?" AJ asked, standing up behind her desk.

A part of her wondered when Gladys would show up next. The problem was that the ghost had expended a lot of energy showing her a vision the day before. Chances were, AJ wouldn't see Gladys for a few days.

Which was too bad. She really could use some backup here.

"Are you familiar with the Milltown app?" Officer Brendan started off with.

Huh. Maybe he was playing "bad cop" that day. Usually, that was Officer Naomi's job.

"I am," AJ said. "Best place for all the news in town."

"Have you been following it recently?" Officer Naomi asked, seemingly surprised.

"Honestly? No," AJ said. "There's been a lot of negativity on the app the last few days, particularly concerning Carla Lowenstein."

Both officers nodded at that. AJ's remark made perfect sense given what was currently being said about her as well as about Carla.

"Are you familiar with the account EarlyRiser?" Officer Brendan asked.

"I saw it for the first time yesterday," AJ replied truthfully.

"Really?" Officer Brendan asked, seeming surprised. "I mean, are you sure?" he asked in a much gruffer voice.

AJ didn't roll her eyes at the man no matter how much she might want to. He made such a lousy bad cop. "Yes, I'm certain. Why do you ask?"

"It's a little suspicious that this EarlyRiser was able to direct the search crew to the exact spot where Carla's body was found. Don't you think?"

AJ shrugged. "If you're trying to imply that I'm EarlyRiser, you're mistaken. I have an account on the app, with my name." She was glad that she'd taken Bea's advice and used her real name, instead of coming up with a fake username.

Not to mention that none of Bea's suggestions would have worked—BossySister or TheOlderOne weren't really appropriate, no matter what Bea said.

"Don't you think it's odd, though, that EarlyRiser created their account the same week you created yours?" Officer Brendan said.

"Really?" AJ said. "I had no idea." She did vaguely recall noticing that the account had been created last May. She hadn't noticed the date, or connected it to her arriving.

"So you're still saying that you aren't EarlyRiser?" Officer Brendan pressed.

"I'm not," AJ said truthfully.

"How do you think EarlyRiser got their information about where Carla's body was?" Officer Brendan said.

AJ tried to shrug nonchalantly. "Maybe they had a vision," she said in an attempt to be cheeky.

"Yet someone else with visions of Carla? That isn't likely, now, is it?" Officer Brendan said.

"You never know," AJ said. "There are ghosts in this town. Maybe there are other oracles as well."

At least at the mention of ghosts, both the officers looked a little less comfortable.

AJ really wished Gladys would show up. It would be a lovely, dramatic moment if all the picture frames on the wall suddenly rattled.

However, the ghost stayed quietly away.

"Who do you think this EarlyRiser is?" Officer Brendan said.

"It's an anonymous account. It could be anyone," AJ said. "Plus, they weren't the only one who claimed to see something in the water in that location, right?"

"That is true," Officer Brendan said, nodding.

AJ tried not to smirk at the glare that Officer Naomi shot him.

"We all know that the body wasn't anywhere near the surface. She was found near the ocean floor, weighted down," Officer Brendan said.

"Really?" AJ said. She actually hadn't known that at all. "That's bad. That means it's murder, right? Not an accident?"

"That's right," Officer Brendan said. He gave her an exasperated sigh. "So you didn't have a vision about the body? Or some other way of knowing about its whereabouts?"

AJ tried to tell the literal truth, because lying, particularly to the police, was never a good idea. (Besides, she'd never been much of a liar. Bea had been much better at it than she'd ever been.)

"I didn't sit down at my scrying bowl in my reading room, at home, and have a vision, no," AJ said clearly. "That's where I have my visions, as well as do my psychic work."

Technically, what she said was the exact truth. Plus, it hadn't been *her* vision. It had been Gladys's. Though why the ghost had felt inclined to help Carla, she'd possibly never know.

The two officers stared at her, then glanced at each other.

AJ could tell they didn't believe her.

Well, crap.

However, instead of pressing her further, Officer Brendan said, "If you have any knowledge about the case that you think is pertinent, such as the identity of this EarlyRiser, you should contact us."

"Even if I have another vision?" AJ couldn't help but ask. Stupid, she knew. But she hadn't been able to stop herself.

Though Officer Naomi rolled her eyes, Officer Brendan replied earnestly, "Yes. Yes. Even then."

The pair of them left and AJ took a deep breath, releasing it with a loud sigh.

That had gone better than she could have hoped.

Still, she had to figure out who it was that had actually killed Carla.

And soon.

Or the next time the police came by, they might not be as friendly.

Chapter Eleven

Yet another card was waiting for AJ when she got home. The card itself was fine, and had a picture of two cartoon giraffes with their necks intertwined, the pair of them holding a heart in their mouths that said, "Happy Valentine's Day!"

All the cards were still weirding her out, though.

AJ didn't bother checking the Milltown app again until later that night, after she'd come home from dinner.

GrayDawn was back, still insisting that AJ must be the killer. She and Carla had been in competition after all. Now that AJ was looking, she realized that GrayDawn appeared to know all about the interaction that AJ had had with Carla, and the vision she'd shared.

Huh. Seamus had only accused AJ of threatening Carla. He'd not mentioned the vision. Had Carla not told her manager all the details?

Who was GrayDawn? Seamus had been Carla's manager, whatever that meant. But GrayDawn might have been closer to her.

AJ texted Bea her questions, not expecting an answer until the next morning. However, Bea replied right away.

Seamus got Carla her big gigs. Check him out

She listed the website for Seamus's business.

Huh. It appeared that Top Talents, Inc. was primarily a booking service. It probably had been Seamus who'd gotten Carla the gig of doing the séance on the cruise ship.

AJ repeated her question to Bea.

And what about GrayDawn?

Again, the reply came immediately.

No one knows

Someone must know. AJ was certain of it. Secrets were too hard to hide in this small town.

Would Seamus know? Should AJ go and talk with him? She looked back at the app. The pair of them did appear to have some sort of connection.

However, Seamus hated her. Thought she was responsible for Carla's death.

Unless some other inspiration struck her, AJ knew she was stuck.

She had to go meet with Seamus. See if she could convince him that she wasn't the killer, despite her lack of alibi.

And hopefully, survive the encounter.

She filled out an inquiry form on his website, truthfully saying that she was a psychic looking to expand her clientele. The site let her pick a meeting time automatically, and as there was a slot the next day, she set herself up an appointment.

She didn't use her initials for the appointment, but rather, her full name, Ariella Jane Steward. (Her mother had given her the choice of being a princess or a plain Jane. AJ had chosen neither, but made up her name instead. Bea had been given a similar choice, and had made a similar decision. If there had been a third child, their mother would have chosen a name that started with C, and possibly just as ridiculous.)

Wednesday morning dawned clear for the first time since the weekend. The tide was in and the bright sunshine sparkled on the waves. Bubbles popped in the sand as the water crept close then receded, showing the location of buried shellfish. Long-legged terns raced along the edge, scooping out tiny minnows from the shore. The wind was strong, but AJ relished heading into it on her short walk that morning.

AJ only worked half a day on Wednesdays, as it tended to be one of the slowest days at the inn. In addition, she had a call with Ursula that afternoon and the meeting with Seamus. Plus clients later on that evening.

Seamus didn't have an office in Milltown, but in the next town up, Sunset. AJ had arranged with Bea to drive her there. One of these days, AJ was going to have to get a new-to-her car. She'd just never found the time, though. Plus, generally speaking, she just didn't need one. Unfortunately, unlike Seattle, there weren't a lot of easy rental car options.

The work at the inn went smoothly, so much better than the day before. Generally, AJ took her time eating lunch these days. She was so *over* bolting her food between meetings, something she'd done for years while working in software in Seattle. However, that Wednesday she just grabbed a sandwich from the Storm Brew Café and rushed back to the house, as she needed to finish eating before her call with Ursula.

Walking up to the house, she discovered that day's card, a basketful of cuddly kitten with the saying, "You're the PURRR-fect Valentine!"

However, for the first time, additional writing appeared on it. Someone had used a marker and written in block letters on the bottom of it, "Have you foretold me?"

AJ felt uneasy as she put the card with the others. Though the card was still cute, the written message felt off to her. It wasn't a threat, but it still felt ominous. She forgot about it, though, in her rush to get ready for dinner with Bea.

Hopefully, come Friday, she'd actually find out who had been sending them, as well as why.

Her mentor had seen all the nastiness on the Milltown app, and had texted AJ a couple of times over the weekend, making sure that she was okay.

So it didn't surprise AJ that the first words out of Ursula's mouth were, "How are you? How are you holding up? Are you okay?"

"I'm fine," AJ told Ursula truthfully. "It's a little hard right now, but it's going to get better." She was certain of that, certain that this wouldn't permanently ruin her reputation. Already, glancing at the app, it felt to her that fewer people were listening to Seamus and GrayDawn.

While AJ didn't wish any harm on anyone, she couldn't wait until something else happened to take the attention away from her and Carla's death.

"That's good. You let me know if you need the big guns to come out and straighten those people up," Ursula huffed.

"No, no, it's fine," AJ insisted. Ursula was actually in her eighties, something that AJ had only recently learned. (She was spry enough that AJ had initially believed Ursula to be in her sixties.) Ursula lived with her sister in Georgia, two batty old spinsters with too many cats—her words, not AJ's.

"So tell me about your latest visions," Ursula said.

AJ complied, telling her about the first vision she'd had of Carla, along with the vision gifted her by Gladys.

She finished up by asking, "Do you know why I'd have such a strange sheen on the water? Both times, before I started?"

"Did you have an urge to have a vision?" Ursula said.

"No," AJ said. Previously, most of her visions had started off with the feeling that something was off, that she *needed* to have a vision.

"Then chances are, that light you're seeing came from something external to you," Ursula said. "I've had something similar happen to me. It sometimes indicates that you're not viewing a regular person, but someone with a gift. Not necessarily a water witch. They may not even know that they have magic."

"That can't be it," AJ said immediately. "Carla didn't have any magic."

"Why are you so certain?" Ursula said.

"Because she was a con artist," AJ insisted. "Carla didn't see the future. Couldn't connect people to ghosts of their past, either."

"Are you sure?" Ursula asked gently. "You've said before that you've found it frustrating not being able to see magic, like they can in the books. That you generally have no idea if someone has any power or not."

AJ gave a great sigh. How did she know that Carla didn't have any power?

Except that, as far as she could tell, it wasn't that Carla didn't have magic.

No, her sureness was all about Carla being able to predict the future.

"All right," AJ said grudgingly after a few moments. "It's possible that Carla did have a type of magic. I have no idea what. I'm certain that it wasn't water magic, that she couldn't see the future."

"Could she talk to ghosts?" Ursula asked.

"I don't know," AJ said. "Maybe? If she could, Gladys's involvement might make more sense."

"Have you had a chance to look at her ghost box?" Ursula said.

"What? No," AJ said dismissively.

Ursula paused before she continued. "Do you believe that the bowl you use for seeing visions will remain immune to you? That after you use it for a few decades, that it won't carry any residue of the magic you're using?"

That made AJ stop and think. "I...I don't know. Maybe?"

"So perhaps there's a chance that Carla, and whatever magic she had, was practiced with that radio," Ursula pointed out. "And it, too, might maintain a hint of it."

AJ sighed as she considered. Yes, Ursula might have a point. While AJ was certain that Carla had primarily been a con artist, maybe she'd also had some power. Some level of magic.

She knew that the radio was important. It had represented Carla in her vision. Plus, now that she was thinking about it, she remembered how the radio had caught at her attention that time she'd gone to see Carla.

"So how do I find out more about her radio?" AJ asked after a few moments.

"Do you think Lionel would let you into her shop? Just for a few minutes?" Ursula said.

"Who?" AJ didn't know a Lionel, did she?

"Lionel Jackson. He's the landlord of that building," Ursula said.

Now that AJ was thinking about it, she did recall meeting a Lionel at one of the chamber of commerce meetings. Tall black man, wearing large, square black glasses, a T-shirt from what looked like a Japanese comic, and a hearty laugh. He'd only attended one of the meetings she'd been at, so she couldn't actually say that she knew him.

"Can you speak to Lionel for me?" AJ asked. While it was important for her to do things on her own, for herself, Bea had been drilling it into her head that she needed to ask for help from other people, even if it made her distinctly uncomfortable.

"Of course!" Ursula said. She sounded delighted. "Lionel and I go way back. I introduced him to his wife!"

"That's good. Thank you," AJ said.

Ursula told her all about the reading she'd given Lionel and how he'd found the missing part of his heart through her. The story warmed AJ considerably.

Hopefully, Lionel would feel obligated to Ursula, and he'd let her into Carla's space.

After AJ said goodbye to her mentor, she didn't have a lot of time to sit and think about what she'd learned. Bea would be there shortly to take her to her meeting with Seamus. (Though Bea was going to be late. She always was.)

Still, AJ felt better after having talked with Ursula. Yes, she might have to change her opinion of Carla. At least a little, as nothing would convince AJ that Carla was an actual oracle.

But there was more, different magic in the world. Ursula only knew about one type.

What other kinds of magic existed? And where was AJ going to learn about them?

AJ considered teasing Bea with, "Are we there yet?" questions on their drive up Highway 101 to the town of Sunset. However, Bea had a different focus, namely, she wanted to pester AJ about magic.

"What do you mean, Carla might have had some sort of magical power?" Bea said, shocked.

"Why are you so surprised?" AJ said. Bea appeared to be really rocked by this concept.

Bea shot her a look despite speeding down the highway. The day had stayed sunny and clear, and not many cars were out. While the trees were still bare, the long days of rain had brightened up the green grass. Ferns were just starting to unfurl. AJ couldn't wait for the signs of spring, and all the different colors of green that would show up.

"It's one thing to know that your weird older sister might have magic," Bea said slowly. "Remember, I did grow up with you. It's something else entirely to start thinking that there might be *other* people with magic as well."

"Ursula has magic," AJ pointed out.

"Not the same," Bea said. "She was already working as a psychic. Do you think that all psychics have some level of power?"

AJ shook her head. "I doubt it. According to Ursula, magic is actually fairly rare." She thought back to Willow, the young woman who worked at reception at the inn. Most of the time, she talked a lot of nonsense and gibberish about the power of the stones and gems she wore, how the goddess spoke to her.

However, there had also been times when she'd been scarily accurate assessing AJ's spirit, claiming to be able to read her aura.

Did such things exist?

Ursula claimed that Willow had no magic at all.

AJ wasn't certain.

Willow might actually have magic, though it was minor compared to what AJ and Ursula could do. Plus, if she did have any, it was a very different type of magic.

"So it's unlikely that anyone else in Milltown has magic, then," Bea said slowly. "That's good."

"Why? Are you prejudiced against people who might have magic?" AJ teased.

Bea answered her seriously, though. "People are never going to be comfortable around magic. Particularly if it's as rare as you say it is. It's unnerving to think about the things you can do, quite frankly."

"Oh," was AJ's only response. She recalled how Bea shivered whenever AJ used her power to dry her off.

"I do *not* want you to stop doing your thing around me, though," Bea added. "Getting dry that quickly is a blessing, not a curse."

"Okay," AJ said. "So you're comfortable with magic if it's useful to you."

"Isn't everyone?" Bea asked, still sounding serious. "No one wants magic to just be cast around willy-nilly."

"I don't know. Sounds like fun," AJ said.

"No, it doesn't," Bea said. "It sounds like chaos."

"Who are you and what have you done with my artistic younger sister?" AJ asked.

Bea shrugged. "Okay, I'll admit that I enjoy a bit of chaos now and again, possibly more than the regular person. But it's still somewhat controlled chaos. Anyone being able to do anything at any time? That just sounds like a recipe for disaster."

"Magic does appear to follow some fairly strict rules," AJ said. "Like water witches. We deal with water. That's about it."

"So what would Carla have been dealing with if this ghost box of hers was real? If she could communicate with ghosts?"

"Air, maybe? Gladys does have quite a chilling effect. And she blows things around all the time, particularly if we leave bits of paper scattered out in the lobby," AJ said.

"Okay," Bea said slowly. "So maybe Carla had an affinity to air. That might make sense."

"Thanks," AJ said dryly. "I have been known to do that now and again."

Bea just rolled her eyes. "And what about Willow?"

"See, I don't get Willow and her possible ability to see auras. What causes an aura in the first place?"

"Heat?" Bea suggested. "So maybe fire?"

"No, I don't think so," AJ said slowly. "She keeps

talking about these gems of hers, and how they have power. Instead of fire, maybe it's earth? And how a person connects with the ground?"

"Either that, or Willow is barking up the wrong tree, like Carla," Bea said. "If Carla's connection was with ghosts and spirits, she shouldn't have been trying to see the future."

"But my connection is with water, yet I still read tarot cards," AJ replied. Her clients had freely given her all sorts of testimonials as to her power with the cards and the readings.

AJ never felt as if she was doing that much with them. She was, instead, letting the cards speak for themselves, watching the flow of symbols.

Maybe that was water as well, getting into the flow of things.

"I don't know about tarot," Bea said. "I know you're good with the cards, but that's also kind of connected to the future. Is water future facing? While air might be past?"

"And maybe earth is present. But then what about fire? What could you do with fire?" AJ mused.

"Besides burn everything to the ground? I don't know." Bea paused, then added, "Almost everything burns. Could fire be the connecting link? The one that joins all the other elements together?"

"That's a scary thought," AJ said. She shivered. "I don't think I'm very interested in meeting someone who is a fire witch, if that's the case."

Bea laughed, and not very politely. "Now you know how I feel when I think about other people having magic."

"All right. You may have a point," AJ said. She paused, looking out at the scenery flowing past.

Flow felt *right* to her. Flowing like water. Finding her way around, through, or under obstacles. Or sometimes splashing over them.

Willow was attracted to her stones, or at least that was what AJ had observed. It might be a bunch of mumbo-jumbo, but there might also be a connection there that Willow wasn't aware of. Plus, she didn't know how to exploit her connection to the earth and its minerals. She didn't have much power either.

Had Carla's element been air? And how was that connected to the past? Though maybe it wasn't the past, per se, but merely ghosts and spirits of the air.

AJ was suddenly looking forward to meeting with Lionel later that evening, after she'd seen her clients. It had been sweet of him to contact her directly after talking with Ursula, though her mentor had warned her that Lionel was going to try to get her to rent the space.

AJ was perfectly happy with the space that she had. Plus, Ursula had kind of insisted that AJ keep the business in the house.

As for fire, was that the connecting element? Did it link to all the others, and therefore have properties of all the others? It really was a disturbing thought.

AJ didn't have anyone she could ask, though, as Ursula didn't know.

For a brief moment, AJ thought she heard the radio come on, playing an old song that she couldn't quite recognize.

When she looked up, she could see that Bea hadn't

turned the radio on. Maybe the car they'd just passed had had their radio turned up high. She pulled out her phone, just to make sure that she hadn't mistaken her ringtone for the radio, but no one had called.

Strange.

After AJ put her phone away, she looked out the window for a short while before she finally turned to her sister and asked, "Are we there yet?"

Chapter Thirteen

Seamus's office, the home of Top Talent, Inc., was located in a generic strip mall just south of Sunset proper on the highway. It didn't look like much of anything, one story and all concrete, with light industrial warehouses on the blocks beside it. The other shops in the strip included an insurance agency, a laundromat, a dog grooming and daycare, and a small dumpling shop that promised to be the best in the area.

AJ wasn't sure how much business any of these stores accumulated. Perhaps it was on the way to someplace else, so people would pass it going from one location to another. It wasn't much of a destination.

Bea shot her a look of concern as they pulled into the mostly empty parking lot, but followed easily enough into the office.

They both stopped for a moment, blinking in the dimness after being in the bright sunlight.

Directly across from the door was a desk with an older woman sitting behind it. The carpet had a distinct moldy smell, the kind that was easy to catch in the Pacific Northwest. A huge world map spread out along the wall leading to a hallway behind the desk, with tons of pins in it.

Client Locations proclaimed the sign above the map.

"Can I help you?" the woman asked grumpily, her voice low and harsh. Based on the nameplate sitting on her desk, AJ would bet her name was Marge. She had curly brown hair that was carefully maintained with judicious application of modern chemicals. A brown-and-gold jeweled chain hung down from the sides of her large glasses. She wore a white-and-gray striped blouse that showed off her ample figure.

"I have a two o'clock appointment with Seamus," AJ said.

"Your name?" Marge asked.

AJ would swear that Marge smoked at least a pack a day, based on how gravely her voice was.

"Ariella Jane," she said.

Bea snickered. AJ shot her a look. Bea just stuck her tongue out at her.

Marge pressed a button on her desk, then waited for a moment. "Seamus will see you now."

When Bea made as if to follow AJ, Marge stopped her.

"Whoa, whoa, whoa," she said pointedly. "One at a time."

"Fine," Bea said. "I'll wait out here."

AJ nodded, and proceeded down the dank hallway alone. She knew that Bea would come running to her rescue if she screamed.

Plus, AJ always carried a bottle filled with water in her purse. She'd practiced pouring it out, then smacking the flow of water with the palm of her hand. It would form an amazingly effective shield, as well as an impressive fist, hitting whatever she needed to hit.

Seamus's door was on the right side, standing wide open. AJ poked her head in and saw Seamus himself sitting behind his desk.

"Come in! Come in," he said, standing up but staying behind his desk, holding out his hand to AJ. "You must be Ariella Jane."

AJ shook his hand. While Seamus had a strong grip, he wasn't trying to overpower her or anything.

The office was very masculine, with square, brown leather guest chairs dotted with brass pins along the edges, the desk itself large and modern with three computer monitors set on it, and the walls covered with posters that AJ was familiar with, advertising local acts and show. It smelled of overly sweet men's aftershave. Of course, it was freezing in there. AJ was glad she was wearing an extra sweater over her office clothes, a silk, dove-gray blouse and a black skirt.

Seamus himself looked fairly ordinary. AJ would put him in his mid-fifties, with kinky black hair that was receding from his forehead as well as shot through with gray, making him look more mad scientist than distinguished gentleman. He had a prominent nose that had been broken in what had surely been a misspent youth, and never fixed properly. Watery blue-green eyes gazed at her with cunning, seeking to gain whatever advantage they could.

"So you're looking to increase your business, eh?" Seamus said. He gave her a frank look up and down. "While the office chic is a good look for you, that isn't what your clients are going to want. They want you to look more mysterious," he said.

"What, like a smoky eye and baggy dress?" AJ said dryly.

"Exactly!" Seamus said. "Those little details will go a long way toward getting you the right sorts of clients, the ones who will pay out."

"What about talent, or magic?" AJ said.

"Fairy tales," Seamus said, dismissing the possibility entirely. "Such things don't really exist. And if you think they do, you're deluding yourself."

"I see," AJ said. And she did. Seamus's clients only deluded their customers. No one else.

"So tell me about yourself. You're a psychic? Where are you operating out of?" Seamus asked.

AJ could tell that the only reason this man asked questions was so that he could then give his input and direct everything. He didn't honestly care about anyone else.

"I'm located in Milltown," AJ answered truthfully.

"Good, good," Seamus said. "That little town could use another psychic. The last one I sent there—Carla Lowenstein—did really well."

"Why did you send Carla to Milltown?" AJ asked, curious. She'd never heard the story as to why Carla had set up shop there.

"There's a growing demand for psychics in this crazy world," Seamus said seriously. "People are all looking for guidance, am I right?"

"I guess," AJ said.

"Exactly," Seamus said, as if AJ had enthusiastically agreed. "Beginning someplace small, like Milltown, can build you a solid reputation. Then, I can start getting you gigs elsewhere. Maybe get a positive connection with the police. Eventually, you'll have to leave Milltown, though. Go to a bigger city. Get more clients, as well as more *important* clients."

AJ had no problem reading that as *richer* clients.

From whom she was certain Seamus wanted a cut.

"So what happened to Carla?" AJ asked.

"Tragic, really," Seamus said. "Seems she got in a feud with the other psychic in town, who threatened her, and..."

Seamus's words trailed off. "You're a psychic. Who lives in Milltown," he said, as if AJ had just now come into his office. "Ariella Jane."

"Yes," AJ said. "AJ Steward."

"What do you want? Why are you here?" Seamus asked. For a few moments he seemed flustered. Then he pulled himself together and leaned over his desk to glare at AJ. "Or are you here to threaten me as well?"

"First of all, I didn't threaten Carla. I had a vision and I told her about it. It wasn't a threat. It was a possible warning. That was all," AJ said firmly.

"Phwww. A warning," Seamus said. "Just a polite way of saying threat."

AJ rolled her eyes. "I did not threaten her. Besides, the vision had symbols, not a dead body. There was a chance it wouldn't have come true, that what I saw could have been altered."

Seamus gave an exaggerated shiver. "Oh dear. You're a true believer," he said softly.

AJ didn't like the calculating look in his eyes. "Who's GrayDawn?" she asked. May as well see if she could get some information out of Seamus before he threw her out of his office.

"Who?"

"GrayDawn? It's the name of a user on the Milltown app. I figured since you two sided with one another that you must know each other," AJ said.

"What, you haven't been able to manufacture a vision about him?" Seamus sneered.

"My talent lies in looking toward the future, not the past," AJ said. "But you do know who GrayDawn is, right? You just said they were a him."

Seamus pressed his lips together and glared at her. "Fine. All right. I do have suspicions about this GrayDawn. But nothing is for free."

"Okay," AJ said. She raised her chin. "What do you want?"

"Do you want to grow your psychic business?" Seamus asked seriously. "I arranged that séance cruise for Carla. I could do something similar for you."

AJ sighed. "I don't do séances. I don't talk with the dead. Usually," she had to amend truthfully.

She talked with a single ghost. That didn't really count, right?

"But you read tarot cards, though?" Seamus asked. "How about a night of card readings?"

AJ nodded slowly. She'd actually thought about doing something like that for her business. "I could do that," she said. "When I opened, I did a series of fifteen minute, three card reads for people for free."

"Smart," Seamus said. "The first one's always free."

AJ didn't roll her eyes at his cynicism, but she thought

about it. Despite the fact that he was kind of spot on—she had given away all those readings in the hopes of gaining more.

They negotiated an agreement, with AJ doing readings on one of the coastal dinner cruises, talking with clients before and afterward. AJ arranged to have a helper with her, who also got the cost of the cruise for free. If Bea wasn't available, she'd have Willow help her.

While they were hammering out the details, AJ would swear that Marge was playing with the office radio. She kept hearing music playing softly in the background. One song would start, fade away, there'd be silence for a while, then another might start.

"I'll have Marge draw up the contracts and send them to you," Seamus said after they'd figured out most of the details, including his percentage of her fee.

"Great," AJ said. "Now, you have something. I still want to know who GrayDawn is."

Seamus gave her his best shark smile.

"He was Carla's boyfriend."

Chapter Fourteen

Bea promised AJ that she'd figure out who this GrayDawn was in a hurry. "Don't you worry," Bea said. "I know exactly who will know this."

"Thank you," AJ said, more grateful than she could express. Though she wasn't always comfortable asking for help, she was getting better at it.

"Now, you go deal with your clients, and text me after you meet with Lionel," Bea instructed.

"All right," AJ said.

Her readings went better than AJ would have guessed, given how busy she'd been and how many other things she had on her mind. Fortunately, they were mostly easy that night.

First was Agnes, an older white woman who looked like a fisherman's wife. She'd been one of the most faithful clients that AJ had inherited from Ursula. The woman wore beat down, ragged clothing—always meticulously clean, but also frayed. However, she owned one of the larger restaurants in the area, and could afford to wear anything she wanted.

Then came Lilly, another client AJ had inherited from Ursula. She was also older and white, possibly close to Ursula's age. While Agnes actually was curious about the future and what she should do next with her business, Lilly needed to talk more than listen. AJ had moved her from a full card reading to just a three card draw, so that they'd have a lot (LOT) more time to discuss not only what the cards said but so Lilly could tell AJ everything that was going on in her life.

Then there was Jamal, a client that AJ had snagged herself. He was a serious young black African-American man studying for law school. Despite Ursula's warning that very few people had any sort of magic, AJ always wondered about Jamal, particularly given her recent conversation with Bea. He held himself so tightly, rarely giving her any reaction.

At some point, AJ was going to ask why he was coming to see her. She suspected it had nothing to do with whatever she said in the cards, but everything to do with stepping outside of himself, if for the shortest of times.

After Jamal left, AJ closed up shop and headed out. The moon was three-quarters full. It wouldn't be quite full by Friday, Valentine's Day, but hopefully there would be clear skies and she'd at least be able to see it.

While AJ didn't believe in all the hoopla about the moon and how it drove magic, she was well aware that, scientifically speaking, the moon was connected to the tides. As she was a water witch, she'd tried experimenting doing magic during different phases of the moon.

However, as far as she could tell, the moon didn't affect her magic at all.

The tides were another matter. At high tide, AJ appeared to be just a smidge stronger than at low tide. It wasn't a huge difference. She had to pay strict attention to even notice it. Ursula had never seen a difference, though AJ suspected her mentor had never experimented that much with it either.

AJ didn't walk down the beach that night—it was still February, and the wind was like a knife, cutting through her outer layers. Instead, she walked down Main Street. Most of the shops were closed—it was the off-season and no one had any reason to be out, despite the lack of rain that day.

It felt as though the wind was seeking her out to chill her that evening, especially since there wasn't anyone else on the street for it to wrap around. Or maybe it was just another hormonal night, and she was going to be colder than usual no matter what she did.

AJ met Lionel on the sidewalk outside the saltwater taffy shop. He was a large, lurking figure, and AJ could easily see how someone might be afraid of him if they didn't know him.

But his smile lit up the street as he saw her, what light there was catching also on his large glasses.

"AJ!" Lionel said, stepping up and holding out his hand. "What a pleasure to meet you again."

"Same here," AJ said, shaking his warm hand with her cold one. "Thank you so much for coming out tonight to show me the store."

"Not a problem!" Lionel assured her. "I have some bread proofing right now, so the timing was perfect."

"Bread proofing?" AJ asked as Lionel fiddled with his keys and unlocked the front door.

"Yeast dough has to rise. So you 'proof' the dough, put it in a warm location so it will rest, giving the yeast time to ferment, which helps the dough rise."

"I see," AJ said, though she barely did. "Are you a cook, then?"

"Baker," Lionel corrected her gently as he flipped on the lights. "I make a mean cinnamon roll. The secret is to get a tight roll, so all that gooey filling spreads everywhere."

"Sounds delicious," AJ said truthfully as she followed the large man up the stairs. Though she was more of a yogurt-and-fruit breakfast type person, she wouldn't say no to some hot, freshly baked cinnamon rolls on occasion.

"They are," Lionel assured her. "I'm not good enough to be on one of those cooking show contests. Not yet, anyway. But someday, I will be."

"Wow," AJ said, impress. "Do you also want to set up your own bakery sometime?"

"I've thought about it. But it's a huge step going from being a home baker to owning a shop," Lionel assured her. "Got to get my recipes just right before I start spreading the sugar around."

"That's so awesome!" AJ told him.

Lionel had paused at the door, considering. He'd unlocked it with his key, but was now staring at the doorhandle. "You know, I could have sworn I'd locked that the last time I left," he said quietly.

A chill went down AJ's back. Before she could say anything or caution him, Lionel pulled the door open.

Chaos greeted them.

AJ pushed past Lionel, who'd stopped in the doorway.

Someone had torn the place apart. After staring at the evidence, AJ determined that they'd been looking for something. The cute pumpkin pillows were all slashed, the stuffing spilled over the floor. Light strings that had been hanging around the window and decorating the wall had been torn down, the hooks carelessly ripped from the wall. There were even holes that had been drilled through the drywall, as if someone had been looking for a secret compartment. The gaudy skirt made of coins that had been on the wall had been shredded, the coins scatted everywhere.

AJ finally tore her eyes away from the mess in front of her to Carla's desk at the side of the room. It was an oasis of clean space considering the rest of the room.

Too clean.

Everything that had been on the desk was now missing. If Carla kept client files, or any business records, AJ would bet those had been taken.

Behind the desk, the ghost box radio was also missing.

AJ turned to look at Lionel, whose dark brown skin had an ashen tone to it.

"I'm sorry," he said, stumbling over the words. "I don't, I never, I just—"

"It's okay," AJ said. "You weren't aware that someone had broken in."

Mutely, Lionel shook his head.

"Who would do this?" AJ asked.

"I don't know!" Lionel said. "Carla was such a dear. Always paid her rent on time. I can't imagine anyone being angry enough to do this!"

AJ shook her head. While there was some anger here, that didn't strike her as the primary emotion. If that had been the case, the chairs would have been tipped over, possibly the desk destroyed. No, it looked as though someone had been methodically looking for something.

What, though? And had they found it?

Lionel pulled out his phone, calling the police, telling them that there had been a break-in.

AJ's heart sank. Another encounter with Officers Naomi and Brendan was pretty much at the bottom of her list of things she wanted to do. Particularly in regard to another crime.

"They'll be here in a while. Seems there's another incident before us," Lionel said. He sighed and shook his head. "Come on. Let's go wait outside for them."

AJ nodded and followed him out to the street. "Do you need to go and tend to your bread? I can wait for the police if you have to make a quick run home."

That at least got her a smile. "No, but you're a dear for offering. I've texted my wife and she'll take care of it. Thank you."

"What other buildings do you own in town?" AJ asked, trying to find something they could talk about.

It turned out that Lionel primarily managed vacation and rental homes in the area. This building was the only retail property that he owned. He did a lot of the maintenance work on his properties himself, and was famous for providing home-baked cookies for his guests.

AJ tried to pay attention to his comments, but found her gut twisting up at the thought of more police.

"You okay?" Lionel said after a while.

"It's just seeing the police again, you know?" AJ said. "They already think I'm involved with Carla's death."

"I got it," Lionel said, nodding. "Why don't you just run home, then? There's no need for me to even mention that you were here. Gideon, who runs the taffy shop, thought he saw someone go up the stairs as he was leaving, but he didn't see anyone when he went looking."

Lionel said that with such conviction that AJ found herself nodding, believing the lie he told. "Are you sure?" she said.

"I am. Go on, now. Shoo."

"If you ever want to stop by and get a reading, it's on the house," AJ replied fervently as she started to back away.

"I may take you up on that," Lionel assured her with a grin.

Feeling immense relief, AJ turned and scurried down the sidewalk. She was at least two blocks away before the police cars rolled by, lights on but no sirens.

Though she felt guilty about leaving Lionel on his own, once he'd gotten over his initial shock, he'd steadied out tremendously.

But now, the mystery of who killed Carla had expanded. Had it been the same person who'd trashed her space, obviously looking for something? Or was it someone else?

And where was the ghost box radio?

AJ didn't understand why she felt it was all connected, but she did.

Hopefully tomorrow would have better news.

Chapter Fifteen

AJ slept fitfully that night, unsurprising given the day's events. She'd shared all her news with Bea, then arranged to take a longer lunch break the next day, as Bea didn't go into details but claimed that she had news as well.

That Thursday morning, the Milltown app was full of news from Lionel, who had posted about the break-in after he'd talked with the police. He announced that all of Carla's files were gone, though he didn't mention that the ghost box was missing.

AJ knew that it hadn't been an act of violence, at least not at first. The person in question had been searching for something.

But what? And why had they taken the ghost box?

AJ felt as though she had more questions than answers, still.

As she put on her coat, she thought she heard music. Strange. Was someone outside, walking on the beach, listening to the radio? That had happened before. But the sound vanished as soon as she put her hand on the door.

It surprised her that when she opened her door, that day's Valentine's Day card fluttered down from where it had been stuck next to the hinge.

AJ reached down to pick it up, then nearly dropped it again. It felt warm and heavy in her hand, weighing more than it should against her fingers.

Looking at the envelope carefully, she didn't see that anything was in it. Nothing but the card.

With misgivings, she slid open the envelope and took out the card.

Again, it was a kid's Valentine's Day card, this time with a goat. The heart-shaped sign that said, "Happy Valentine's Day!" on it had a couple of bite marks taken out of it.

Again, someone had added their own message. It said, "You will be mine."

That...was threatening.

Should she call the police? Before, the cards every day felt like a weird, badly executed prank.

This felt like something more.

AJ took a picture of the card from that day as well as the day before, then found the information for Officer Brendan. She sent him a quick email from her phone, explaining how she'd been receiving cards every day and that the pictures were from the last two.

She didn't expect to get an email back right away, and she didn't. Instead, she got through her paperwork at the inn, her meetings with Rosita, Sooli, and Payne, then eventually escaped.

The sunshine had deserted the town and once again storm clouds filled the sky. It had been raining off and on all morning, though as AJ was walking to lunch, she'd say it was merely a heavy mist, just enough to warrant something covering her head, but not much else.

The day's special at the Storm Brew Café was home-made tomato soup served with a grilled cheese panini sandwich. It sounded perfect and AJ ordered it immediately, not bothering to wait for Bea.

Her sister was late, as always, and AJ was glad that she'd already started on her lunch. The rain must have started again, because Bea practically squelched when she sat down.

"Oh!" she said, looking at AJ's plate. "I ordered that as well."

"It's good," AJ assured her. "Really good."

Bea looked thoughtful. "You said you saw Carla's office last night, with Lionel?"

"Shhh," AJ said, looking around the café. No one was listening to them, but it was still better that they kept their voices down.

Bea rolled her eyes. However, she did nod, and repeated her question much more quietly.

AJ nodded. "Yeah. It was a mess. Someone had obviously been looking for something. They took all her files, as well as the ghost box."

"Do you think it was the same person as the one who killed Carla?" Bea said.

"Possibly? I don't know," AJ said. Though that was what her intuition said, she had nothing to base it on. After Bea's food was delivered to the table, AJ had to ask, "Did you have any luck finding out who GrayDawn was?"

"Sort of," Bea said. "Did you know that the owner of the app is Jermaine?"

"The guy who runs the electronics store?" AJ said.

"Yup. I don't know if you remember, but when you sign up for the app, you have to provide a mailing address, to prove that you live here," Bea said.

AJ nodded. She'd been able to use Bea's address as hers. After she'd signed up for the app, she received her initial password in the mail.

"Turns out that the address that GrayDawn used is a post office box," Bea said. "The name's obviously a fake—he just used A. Resident—but the PO box is real."

"How in the world did you manage to get that information?" AJ said, awed.

"Jermaine owed me a favor," Bea said. "And no, you don't want to know what."

"Is it like the favor you owed to Jacques?" AJ asked. There still wasn't enough brain bleach in the world to completely erase the nude painting she'd seen of her sister.

"Very similar," Bea said with a coy smile.

AJ gave an exaggerated shudder. "Ugh. So, at least we know where GrayDawn gets his mail."

"Which isn't much," Bea said. "I don't have a way to find out who the person behind that box is. Not without staking out the post office."

AJ sighed. It was something of a lead, but not much.

"So I thought as soon as we finished lunch, we'd go to the post office. Just to see if whoever owns box sixty-one fetches their mail. It is delivered every day around lunch time," Bea said.

"All right," AJ said, a little grumbly. She would much rather sit and digest her food, drink her coffee and chat with Bea, than go back out.

The sisters ate and talked, but they ran out of ideas.

The rain, of course, was much stronger after lunch, sheets of water pounding down on them. While AJ didn't mind the water that much, even she felt bedraggled by the time they reached Bea's car. Fortunately, she was able to dry them off quickly once they got into the car.

The post office was on the southern side of town, tucked up on the hill. It was a modern building, from the 1990s. There was a small counter to the left of the door, slots for accepting mail directly across from the door, and to the right, a wall of boxes that continued around the corner.

Bea told AJ, "This may take a while," as she went to stand in line behind three other people.

AJ looked at her sister, uncertain what to do.

"You could always go look around," Bea said. "While I'm waiting here."

It took AJ a few moments to process what Bea was saying.

"Got it," AJ said. "I'll just be walking around. Trying to get my steps in," she said, holding up her wrist and indicating the fitness watch that she always wore. Since coming to Milltown, she hadn't been at its beck and call as much. The inn kept her on her feet more, and walking to and from town had also been good.

Plus, though she felt as if she'd been eating more food, it had been healthier food overall, despite what her sister thought of the lack of vegetables in her diet.

So AJ deliberately stepped away from Bea, called up her numbers on her watch, then walked to the end of the row of boxes, turned, and kept walking.

Ah ha. Box number sixty-one was in the top row of boxes, about a third of the way down the wall.

AJ walked down to the far end of the post office, then slowly walked back, up to Bea, and down along the boxes again. She made sure to frequently check her watch, knowing that she looked a little weird doing this.

Then again, she was a psychic. The people in Milltown should expect weird behavior from her, right?

At least there were some interesting photos on the wall. Though the post office was currently in a modern building, that hadn't always been the case. There were old black and white photos of the previous buildings where the post office had been located, including what was now someone's home.

AJ wished she had Roland there. She was certain he could tell her the history and stories behind the post office's moves, and make it interesting. While the photos on the walls looked cool, they didn't tell enough of a story.

When Bea finally made it up to the counter, she dawdled, talking to the guy behind the desk, asking about the sizes of boxes that she could rent, how much they cost, how often she'd have to pay, etc.

That gave AJ more time to walk and keep an eye on box sixty-one.

However, no one came by the entire time Bea kept the clerk busy.

Finally, Bea finished her "business" and met AJ beside the boxes. "I think this size of box will be too small for me, don't you think?" Bea said, taking her sister around the corner and pointing to one of the smaller boxes at the top of the stacks.

"I agree," AJ said. "Particularly if you mean to get

supplies delivered here. I would think one of the bigger boxes at the bottom would suit you better."

"That's a thought," Bea said slowly. "I hadn't even considered getting my supplies delivered here!"

The sisters loitered for a little longer, but eventually, AJ told Bea that she had to get back to the inn.

A young man held open the door for them as they left. AJ had an impression of light-colored hair that had been dyed an unnatural dove-gray. It had blue streaks running through it. He also had sharp features and long, skinny fingers.

AJ felt a shiver of *something* as she walked past him.

And she must be hearing things, or someone was playing the radio really loudly in their car, because she would swear she heard music again suddenly.

What in the world?

The rain was coming down in sheets. Bea hurried toward the parked car.

AJ stayed where she was for a few more moments, looking back into the post office.

Was that box sixty-one that the young man had gone to? AJ thought so, but she wasn't certain.

There was a second set of doors at the rear of the post office. The young man went out those, then walked away, not bothering to get in a car.

Which meant he lived nearby, but where?

AJ finally shook it off, slowly returning to the car, where Bea was waiting for her.

"That was him," AJ said with finality.

"Who? That young guy? GrayDawn?"

AJ nodded slowly.

"Well, crap," Bea said. She drummed her thumbs on the steering wheel. "No one at the post office is going to tell us who their client is."

"I know," AJ said. "And...well, I forgot to tell you something." She got out her phone and explained about the last two Valentine's Days cards that she'd received, showing Bea the writing on each.

"That's getting really creepy," Bea said.

"You'll be happy to know that I've already sent these along to Officer Brendan," AJ said, checking her email, then groaning. "Who now wants me to come to the police station this afternoon."

"You want to go now?" Bea asked.

"Yeah," AJ said, sighing. She texted Willow, who was on the front desk at the time, that she'd be late.

She'd make it up to everyone later.

Or so she promised herself—that there would be a later for her.

Chapter Sixteen

Bea first drove AJ to her house to pick up the cards she'd received, then she dropped AJ off at the front of the police station. Though Bea had volunteered to come with her, AJ had insisted on doing this alone.

She was going to the police for help this time. They should be on her side.

Right?

The police station had been built in the 1950s, and looked it. It was short and squat, with mean-looking windows and a single, solid gray door that was probably bomb-proof. Inside the first door was a short entranceway and a second set of doors, also solid looking. There wasn't any glass in the metal doors to see who was coming in, but there was more than one security camera pointed at her from the ceiling.

AJ pulled open the second set of doors and walked up to the desk. At least it was vaguely cheery in here, the counters and the walls painted a bright yellow with dark blue trim. The air stank of burnt coffee. AJ was glad she'd dried herself off some, as it felt as though someone had the AC turned on high, despite the fact that it was February.

An older white woman AJ hadn't met stood behind the counter, dressed in a police officer's uniform. Her nametag read "Toni."

"Can I help you?" the woman—presumably Officer Toni—asked. She had curly white hair that still held onto its original black in places. She looked more like a friendly school librarian than an officer of the law. She had green glasses perched on her nose, magnifying the dark brown eyes behind them, a mischievous smile, and the perfect amount of makeup.

"I'm here to see Officer Brendan," AJ said. "He's expecting me."

"I'll let him know you're here," Officer Toni said.

Officer Brendan walked up to the front with the other woman to meet AJ.

"Hi there," he said with his big, goofy grin. "So glad you could come by. Let's go talk in the conference room," he said, indicating a room to the side. As he held open the door, he said, "I'm going to offer you coffee, but I'm also going to recommend that you don't take me up on it. It's pretty bad. I swear, Toni can burn water."

AJ snorted quietly and assured Officer Brendan, "It's okay. I'm still full from lunch."

The conference room could easily hold twenty people at the long oval table that took up the center of it. Chairs were scattered haphazardly around the table, with three piled up in the corner. The color scheme of yellow and blue had continued in here, though the table itself was white pine. It was as cold in here as it was in the outer office. AJ pulled her coat more tightly around her.

"Tell me about the cards you've been receiving," Officer Brendan said.

AJ explained about the cards, how they'd been appearing every day in February, how they'd always been wedged in between the door and the frame. She spread them out across the table so that Brendan could see them.

"Except for the last couple, I hadn't bothered to keep the envelopes," she explained, handing him one. It was probably the original envelope that had come with the card, cheaply made out of thin paper.

Officer Brendan spent a little time staring at the cards. He picked them up and held them up to the light, saying, "Huh."

"What is it? What do you see?" AJ asked.

"It isn't obvious, but someone has put a very small hole through the eyes of each character on the cards," Officer Brendan said.

"That's...disturbing," AJ said. She picked up one with a cute beaver on it, then held the card up to the light. He was right—the eyes had a very careful pinprick in the center of each. It had been made with a very fine-tipped point so the hole was difficult to see.

"It is disturbing," Officer Brendan said, nodding.

"What do I do?" AJ asked, perplexed. "Is this someone coming after me? Some sort of stalker?"

"Who doesn't want you to see too much? Maybe," Officer Brendan said. "And you haven't had any visions about the cards?"

"None," AJ said, confused. "And honestly, I would

expect that I would if there were something threatening to me going on."

Officer Brendan shook his head. "I don't know. As these have all been sent anonymously, we can't give you any sort of restraining order. Not that those are horribly effective to begin with. You might want to install some sort of camera on your door, to see who comes and goes."

"That's a thought. However, tomorrow's Valentine's Day," AJ pointed out. "I'm assuming that whatever this person wants, they're going to come for it tomorrow."

"Oh, yeah, that's right," Officer Brendan said. "Uhm, are you going to be alone?"

"I have a date, actually," AJ said. "Roland Jax and I are going out to dinner after I finish work."

"Good, good," Officer Brendan said. He paused, then asked, "Is it possible that Roland is sending you these cards?"

"No," AJ said. "I asked him and he didn't lie to me."

Officer Brendan looked skeptical at that, but didn't push. Instead, he asked, "You have my number, right? So you can call if anything goes wrong. Day or night. I'll pick up the phone for you."

Officer Brendan was so earnest that AJ would have wondered if he was hitting on her, except that she recalled that some of the gossip around town was that he didn't necessarily like women.

"How's it going with Carla's investigation?" AJ asked.

"I can't talk about an ongoing case," Officer Brendan said sternly. Then he gave her his usual cheeky grin. "I'm always happy to hear if you have information for us, though. Like a vision."

"Are you familiar with GrayDawn? One of the anonymous users on the Milltown app?" AJ asked.

"I am," Officer Brendan said slowly, nodding. "That person isn't thrilled about you."

"According to Seamus, Carla's business manager, GrayDawn is, or rather was, Carla's boyfriend," AJ said.

"Yeah," Officer Brendan said. "Greg Palmer."

As he said the name so casually, AJ assumed that it must be common knowledge who Carla's boyfriend was, though Seamus hadn't been able to tell her his name.

"Do you know anything about Greg?" Officer Brendan said.

"Just his PO box," AJ admitted truthfully.

"Though he's stayed active on the Milltown app, he hasn't been in town recently," Officer Brendan. "We haven't been able to talk with him in person."

"Huh," AJ said. "I would swear that I just saw him at the post office. Skinny young man, long fingers, hair dyed gray with blue streaks?"

"That's him," Officer Brendan said. "We might have to go pay another visit to his house if he's back in town. He told us that he wouldn't be returning to Milltown for another week."

"Is he a suspect?" AJ asked.

Officer Brendan narrowed his eyes at her. "You know I'm not supposed to discuss an active case with you," he said, sounding a little gruff. He sighed, then sat back in his chair. "He has an alibi, but it isn't air-tight." He paused, then pointed a finger at her. "And you never heard that from me."

"Keep poking into this GrayDawn's background," AJ said. "I have a feeling about him."

"Anything you'd like to share?" Officer Brendan said.

AJ shook her head. "Just...Unsettled. You know?"

Officer Brendan shrugged. "I'll take your word for it. You be careful the next few nights, all right? I don't want to have to go tell Bea that you got in trouble on my watch."

"I will be," AJ said. "And do go look at Greg Palmer again."

"We will," Officer Brendan promised.

AJ had to slog her way back to the inn through the rain. She figured it was probably good exercise for her, as her clothes gained twenty pounds of water weight in the continual downpour.

Why did she have such a bad feeling about Greg Palmer? What was it about him that unsettled her so much?

And why did she keep hearing music in the background? Was this just another (joyous) menopause symptom for her to deal with? Was she just going so crazy that now she was hearing things?

AJ felt as though she had more questions than answers.

And that Valentine's Day was a deadline that she was going to miss.

Chapter Seventeen

After AJ got back to the inn and had dried herself off some, she texted Bea about Greg Palmer as well as the mutilation that had been done to the Valentine's Day cards she'd been receiving.

Unfortunately, Bea didn't know anyone by that name. She didn't even know any Palmers in the area. She promised to do more hunting, though.

The afternoon had a lot of people checking in—seemed that quite a few people came to the coast to spend Valentine's Day. The inn had offered a romantic weekend getaway package, with time in the bathhouse as well as Payne's Valentine's evening meal.

Next year, AJ was going to see if she could talk Lionel into making cookies for her guests as part of the romantic weekend getaway package, giving him a chance to practice his baking and decorating skills.

After the initial flurry of people midafternoon, AJ and Willow found themselves in a lull.

AJ was never certain what to talk about with the

younger woman. When she'd been working in business, she'd always found connection points with her developers. But while those people hadn't necessarily been in competition with her, Willow usually acted as if she and AJ were.

Today, Willow was in her usual man-ish white shirt, black vest, and black pants. She'd shaved the one side of her head recently enough that it was barely stubble, while the other side—done in an ombre of dark red to bright pink— hung down to her shoulder. Her nose ring was plain gold today, though she frequently had some sort of gemstone impaling it. She wore her usual assortment of talismans and stones wrapped around her neck, held there by various leather strips.

"Tell me about the stones you're wearing today," AJ said, trying to keep an open mind about Willow's obsessions.

"This is tiger eye," Willow said, lifting a large, teardrop shaped stone, colored in brown with golden spots. "It's to help me find balance between the fire of inspiration and the grounding of the earth."

"So it's an artist's stone?" AJ said, trying to keep the conversation going, to see what else Willow might or might not know about the various rocks she wore.

"Yes, it could be," Willow said seriously. "Or it could be a transition supporter, if you're going through some sort of change."

"What else are you wearing?" AJ said, determined to find some sort of connection.

Willow went through many of her rocks, the snowflake obsidian, the topaz, and the pure quartz that had so little coloration it was like plain glass, talking about the properties of each, what they were used for magically and internally.

"Where did you learn about all of this?" AJ said after a while.

"All over the place," Willow admitted. "I have several books I could loan you, if you were interested."

"Thanks," AJ said sincerely. "I appreciate that. But rocks just aren't my thing, you know? I prefer water and movement. That flow."

"Then why ask?" Willow said pointedly. While she'd been animated talking about her necklaces, she abruptly fell back into her sullen self.

"There are many types of magic," AJ said seriously. "Not everyone is water based, like I am."

"Oh," Willow said, as if she hadn't ever considered that before. "So while you're water, I might be earth?" She paused for a moment, thinking. "Huh," she finally said.

"Any insight you want to share?" AJ asked.

"No, just that I think you might be right. I need to stay focused on the earth and her bones, not flitting around with other elements," Willow said, nodding.

"Yes, exactly," AJ said.

Willow gave her a considering look. "I know you're a psychic and all," she said, waving a dismissive hand. "But I figured you didn't believe in any of it. That it was just another business for you."

AJ tilted her head from side to side. "Gladys would make a believer out of anyone."

Willow snorted. "True. Enough pictures fall from your walls and either you're living in an earthquake zone or something else is going on."

"Exactly," AJ said. She didn't feel comfortable enough to share anything more with Willow about her magic, to tell her about the visions or pushing around water.

Besides, she still had no idea how much power Willow might have with her chosen element, if any.

"Ursula isn't earth based either, is she?" Willow asked after a few moments.

"No, she isn't," AJ said, wondering where Willow was going with all of this.

"Oh," Willow said after a few moments of consideration.

A guest came up to the desk just then. AJ took care of them and checked them in while Willow continued to work through whatever it was she was considering.

Finally she said, "That's why Ursula wouldn't take me as a student, isn't it?"

"Yes, exactly," AJ said, relieved that she wasn't going to have to say anything about Willow's lack of actual power. "She isn't earth based. And you are."

"That means you can't teach me either," Willow concluded with a nod.

"That's right. I don't know who can. If there's anyone," AJ continued. She didn't want to send Willow down the path of looking for some kind of "teacher" who would in the end turn out to be even more of a con artist than Carla.

"So we end up teaching ourselves, and possibly never learning our true power," Willow said after a few moments, more to herself than to AJ.

AJ just shrugged. She, too, would like a teacher, a better mentor than Ursula. Particularly one versed in all the various types of magic in the world.

Did such a person exist? Maybe. Maybe not.

"It's not like we can put out an ad on the internet or something," AJ said. "And get anyone who has real power, that is."

Willow gave her a grimace. "I know that too well," she said quietly.

AJ heard the heartache barely masked by the young woman.

Someone had taken advantage of her, that was certain.

Still, AJ knew she couldn't take Willow on as a student. They had different magic.

By the time AJ's day was over, she felt as if she and Willow had finally come to something of an understanding. While AJ still didn't know if Willow had any magical power, at least they'd made progress toward figuring out how to work together.

Willow was probably always going to be jealous of AJ, as the young woman had always felt it was her place to be the magical one.

Maybe now, though, she could grow into her own powers, explore what it meant to be earth based, instead of reaching for things that would always be beyond her grasp.

# Chapter Eighteen

AJ didn't have any clients that evening, so she and Bea had made plans earlier to have dinner together in Bea's vacation home up the hill. Though it was still raining, AJ walked up there from the inn, knowing she could dry herself later.

Bea opened the door almost immediately after AJ knocked.

"Why didn't you text me that you were on your way?" Bea said angrily as AJ stood just inside the doorway, magically pushing all the water off herself so she was dry again.

"Why would I do that?" AJ said. "We made an agreement to have dinner tonight. When I got off work. Remember?" Had Bea forgotten or something?

"Yes, but that was before you found out that someone was out to get you, sending you mutilated Valentine's Day cards," Bea fussed.

"I was perfectly fine," AJ said. "I was walking in the rain, remember? I could have protected myself if someone tried to grab me off the street."

Bea was only slightly mollified. "I'll grant you that, but

what if they grabbed you before you had a chance to react? I just—I wouldn't forgive myself if something happened to you."

AJ took a deep breath, ready to tell her sister off, then released it.

Bea might be right. Something strange was going on. Someone was obsessed with her. And not in a good way.

"Okay," AJ said grudgingly. "I'll try not to be alone for the next couple days. All right?"

"Good, I was hoping you'd say that," Bea said with a grin. "We need to go to your place and pick up some of your things. You're spending the night here."

"What?" AJ said, affronted. "Look, Bea, I appreciate it—"

"What did you just say about not being alone for the next couple of days?" Bea pointed out mercilessly.

"Fine," AJ huffed. "I'm sure this isn't necessary, though."

"Oh, I don't know," Bea said coyly. "There might be some alcohol involved. And you might not be able to make it home later tonight anyway. You'll be happy that you agreed to my very sensible plan."

AJ just rolled her eyes at Bea. "You win. Let's go to my place, get some of my stuff, then come back here."

"See? You should always listen to me," Bea said. Possibly just a little pompously.

AJ shook her head but followed her sister back out into the rain, heading for her car. It didn't take long after they reached AJ's place for her to put together an overnight bag. At least no card had been wedged into the door that evening. She wasn't actually expecting the last one until the big day, tomorrow.

Nothing looked weird or out of place. AJ didn't have an unsettled sense when she walked in as if someone had been there while she'd been out.

She wished there was some sort of magic that she could use to protect her house. The best she could come up with would be a moat. Some sort of water feature, that maybe someday she could enchant, that would protect her.

Maybe.

AJ refused to be cowed, though, so she spent a little extra time checking things out, making sure that she was as safe as she thought she was in her own house.

Finally, they were on their way back up the hill to Bea's place. As AJ had spent the first few months of her time in Milltown living in Bea's guest room, it felt comfortable to her, and she already knew where everything was.

After dinner (a marvelous beef stew that Bea had made was both homey and comforting) and dessert (a decadent chocolate pudding with caramel sauce that AJ had picked up), the sisters sat down in the living room to chat, each with a large glass of wine.

"I know better than to ask this, but is there any chance I could get you to leave Milltown for a while? Just until the police find whoever killed Carla?" Bea started off with.

AJ sighed. "You know I can't. The police have specifically asked me not to go anywhere. Plus, if the same person who killed Carla is the person who's been sending me cards, I won't be their only victim. They'll move on to someone else if I leave town. I couldn't live with that."

"I know," Bea said, her own sigh much more emotive.

"So do you think it isn't the boyfriend? This Greg Palmer, or GrayDawn?" Bea said. She continued, on a roll. "We need to figure out who this boyfriend is, what his angle is. Did he believe Carla was a psychic? Is he out to get you because he thinks you're a fake? I mean, why else poke holes in your eyes?"

AJ just shrugged. She, too, had more questions than answers at this time. "It could be that whoever's sending the cards thinks I *am* a psychic. He could be poking holes in the eyes to blind me."

Bea shivered. "That's really psycho. And I'm sure it's going to thrill Fred, who will certainly put it into his next murder mystery."

AJ nodded.

"Maybe there's a clue in GrayDawn's posts," Bea said. "Let's spend some time going through them, see if we can catch anything."

"All right," AJ said. She didn't want to get too obsessive herself, but it still sounded like a good plan.

Bea copied out all of GrayDawn's posts into a file, then printed out two copies, one for AJ and one for herself.

AJ started with the first few posts of GrayDawn, who'd joined the app just after the first of the year. She knew that Carla had set up shop in January. When had Carla actually arrived in Milltown, though?

She sent Lionel a quick text, asking when Carla had first started renting from him.

He replied quickly, letting her know that Carla had signed all the lease papers the previous year, and had gotten the keys on January first.

So Carla had been in Milltown over the holidays. Interesting.

AJ pulled up her phone and found that Carla's account had been set up on the Milltown App in December.

Had GrayDawn followed her from somewhere else?

There was never anything personal in GrayDawn's texts. He never posted about his own hobbies or things he'd done. The first week, he was only forwarding Carla's posts.

It wasn't until the second week that he started making personal attacks against AJ, accusing her of being a "faux psychic" and calling all of her followers delusional.

AJ hadn't seen any of these posts. Fortunately, there weren't many of them. After the first few there were a series of posts that said, "Deleted by Admin."

Had GrayDawn been saying even worst things about her? And had Jermaine stepped in to stop them?

After that, GrayDawn's posts were more subtle. He never said anything directly bad about AJ. Instead, they were almost always about Carla, the only "real" psychic in town who could foretell the future.

Why was GrayDawn so adamant that Carla was the real thing? AJ was still convinced that she'd been a con artist.

There were also a few posts from GrayDawn about Carla's ability to talk with ghosts through her radio. He didn't appear to think that was as impressive a feat, even though that might have been the only real magic that Carla had.

When AJ started reading those posts, she thought for a moment that she heard a radio again. She looked up sharply, but Bea was still sitting there, going through her own copy of GrayDawn's posts.

AJ shook her head. She was hearing things. She'd read more than one story about women going crazy from menopause. This must be her own very special brand of it.

By the time AJ finished reading through all of Gray-Dawn's posts, she didn't have any solid conclusions beyond that he was kind of creepy, always following Carla around, posting how she'd had lunch at the Cove and everyone should go there, or shopping at Fred's store, and the specials they had.

It was only her second time through that she noticed the pattern: he only posted when Carla left her business to go out. He also commented on the times she'd called for food to be delivered. But that was it. As if he was sitting outside her business, stalking her.

That made AJ curious, and she started trolling through Carla's posts.

At the very start, she'd liked his posts, particularly when he'd started forwarding everything she said.

Those likes stopped after the posts that the admin had deleted. After that, Carla never appeared to interact with GrayDawn.

"You know, I'm getting the feeling that GrayDawn wasn't so much her boyfriend as her own personal stalker," AJ said after a bit.

"I gotta say, I agree with you," Bea said. "But Seamus said GrayDawn was her boyfriend?"

"As did Officer Brendan," AJ said, nodding slowly. "I wonder if the nature of their relationship had changed and she hadn't admitted it to anyone."

"Or she was scared to," Bea said.

"I'm sure that the police already know all of this, right?

That they've been looking at these posts?" AJ asked. "Officer Brendan said he was familiar with GrayDawn, and appeared to already know that it was Greg Palmer."

"Yeah, but there wasn't anything they could do, not unless Carla had sworn out a complaint or something," Bea said.

AJ put the papers to the side and finished off her glass of wine. "I wonder what the real relationship was between them."

Bea shrugged. "You're the psychic. You tell me."

AJ shook her head. "I still primarily see the future. Not the past."

"And you haven't had any visions about this?" Bea asked.

"I haven't," AJ said.

"Maybe you should try again," Bea said pointedly.

"Maybe I should." AJ didn't feel compelled to have a vision, but she could always stop if her head started to hurt.

"See? You should always listen to me."

AJ just rolled her eyes and got up to go prepare.

Chapter Nineteen

AJ rejected Bea's offer of the large bowl she usually used for popcorn as her scrying dish. She didn't need that big of a container to hold the water she was going to use. While her own scrying bowl at her house was good sized, just a small cereal bowl would do. Besides, the plastic of the bigger bowl smelled like melted butter, which was distracting.

Bea still fought AJ and her choice of scrying bowl. She snatched away the cereal bowl and replaced it with a fancy, cut-glass serving bowl.

"I want to see if there's extra sparkle," Bea said. "I've watched you have a vision before and I couldn't see anything."

There might have been some extra pouting after that statement.

"Sorry," AJ said. She wasn't.

AJ had only once tried to have a vision in front of a client. That hadn't gone too well. Then again, this was Bea, her sister. Maybe it would be okay.

AJ sat at the kitchen counter and prepared herself

mentally, doing her deep breathing exercises and letting the world fall away. She picked up a couple of wine corks that she comfortably held in her hand, things she could drop into the water to end the vision.

Bea sat quietly to one side, out of AJ's direct line of vision. She'd promised to stay quiet and not distract AJ.

AJ had to think a few minutes about the actual question she needed to ask. She already had a good idea who GrayDawn was. She didn't know where Greg Palmer was, and she wasn't sure that even knowing that would be necessary.

"What does GrayDawn have planned? Show me. Show me his plans. What is planned? What is coming? Show me. Show me his plans."

The chant didn't feel as natural as usual. AJ found it more difficult to slide into the flow of things. Possibly that was because Bea was there, but it might also have been her own uncertainty about what to ask to see.

Finally, wisps of fog covered the water of the bowl in front of her. She thought she heard Bea gasp, but she couldn't afford to look, couldn't break her concentration.

The fog cleared and the water shone, mirror-like.

It was an image of her house, from the vantage point of the ocean, as if AJ was standing out on the water, looking directly east. It was early, the sun had just come up. Gray clouds covered the sky, not allowing much light through. The usual hard winds buffeted her from all sides.

AJ wondered what she was supposed to see there. Everything looked clear. She didn't have any bad feelings about her house. Nothing ominous surrounded it.

It wasn't until she looked to the south that she saw a

black cloud, moving at unnaturally high speeds, coming her way. It was maybe three feet across. The black cloud was wreathed in lightning, crackling and sizzling. She could smell the ozone of its discharge.

The winds suddenly died as the black cloud drew near. It positioned itself directly over her house, then struck the roof with small veins of lightning. They didn't do any damage that AJ could see. Her house was easily able to withstand these attacks.

The black cloud grew agitated, the pieces of it roiling together. The lightning strikes grew heavier but the house remained unharmed.

The strikes stopped for a few moments.

AJ felt the cloud gathered itself together.

Then a *huge* fireball came searing down. It was at least as big across as the house. It was as if fireworks suddenly went off, bigger and brighter sparks of light wreathing her house from roof to ground.

The intensity of the light grew so strong AJ had to look away for a moment.

When she looked back, her house was gone. All that remained was the black cloud, floating smugly over the empty space.

AJ heard a splash under her feet. She looked down toward the water. When she looked back up, she was back in Bea's kitchen.

Bea handed AJ a glass with more wine in it. AJ gulped back the warm liquid, but she was still shivering inside.

GrayDawn was coming for her.

And he wouldn't be satisfied until he'd destroyed her.

AJ sat and drank coffee at the breakfast bar with Bea the following morning. She was listening to Bea tell her, yet *again*, that she needed to leave town.

"That won't work," AJ said, aware that she was repeating herself. "What if Carla had done that exact same thing? Tried to leave Greg? But he followed her up here anyway?"

Bea huffed in frustration. "But you don't have to do the psychic thing, do you? You could go do something else. Be a manager, boss people around again. Just do it somewhere else."

AJ rolled her eyes. "Don't know if that would work. No, this GrayDawn person—Greg—is out to get me. And he won't be satisfied until he destroys me."

"You should go to the police," Bea said, trying a new tactic.

"For a vision? Sure, they're going to help me if I tell them that," AJ said derisively.

"Officer Brendan might," Bea said stubbornly.

AJ shook her head. "I know he might *want* to do something. But there isn't anything he can do." She put her coffee down and stood up. "Come on. Or I'm going to be late to work."

"Are you sure you want to go home first? Before work? I mean, what if he's there or something?" Bea asked.

"If we go to the house first, you'll be with me," AJ said. "The pair of us can take care of him."

Bea glared at AJ. "What if I don't wanna go?" she asked in one of her more bratty voices.

"Then I'll go by myself," AJ said.

"But then you'll be late to work," Bea pointed out.

AJ shrugged. "So be it."

Bea gaped at her for a moment. "Who are you and what have you done with my anal-retentive sister who's a slave to her schedule?"

"Come on," AJ said. "Get a move on."

It still took Bea more time than AJ would have liked to get herself ready to drive AJ first to her house, then to the inn.

AJ wasn't about to admit how worried she was about her home. Had something happened to it last night? Was it still okay? The police would have called her or something if it had burned down, right?

However, the house looked fine as they approached it. Nothing seemed amiss.

The only thing that troubled AJ was the white envelop she could see sticking out from the door frame, tucked in there by some unseen hand.

"He's been here already," AJ said, pointing out the damning white square as Bea stopped the car.

"I see that," Bea said, sounding more sour than their mother after a failed negotiation.

AJ opened the car door and hopped out before Bea could do something like turn around and head back home.

After a few moments, Bea turned off the engine and got out of the car as well. "I'm going to make you pay for my therapy if that card is really gross or creepy."

AJ snorted. "I'm sure Peter will be happy to sign you up for some extra sessions."

"Fine," Bea huffed.

AJ walked from the street up to the front of the house, Bea following a few steps behind.

Nothing seemed amiss with the front of the house: the white picket fence was untouched by graffiti; her garden—and the flowers in it—remained untrampled by angry feet; a little sand had blown across the walkway, but that was usual.

She didn't see any footprints in the sand, which didn't mean much. The wind here was always so strong that her own footprints would be blown away after an hour or so.

AJ checked the lock on the door. It was still solidly closed.

She opened the door and let the envelop flutter down to the threshold, rather than try to tug it out.

Glancing around the entranceway, everything inside looked normal enough. No one was there, or had been there.

AJ hesitated before she reached for the card at her feet. She still had the sense that the card was heavier than usual, as if the message within was weighty.

Bea picked up the card by the edges, careful to not touch the places where there might be fingerprints. "Let's see what the midnight postman brought, shall we?"

AJ nodded. They both entered the house. She closed and locked her front door behind them, then gingerly took the card from Bea, also handling it just on the edges.

This envelop, like the others, was made from thin paper. The flap wasn't gummed, nor was it tucked inside the rest of the envelop.

AJ shook the envelop, letting the card drop out onto her front entrance table.

The picture was similar to all the others, with cartoon characters. For the first time, instead of cartoon animals, they were people, an old man and an old woman, him bald, her with an old-fashioned bun. Their poses were exaggerated as they bowed toward one another, their butts in the air, heads out, seeking a kiss. The silhouette of the pair of them suggested a heart.

AJ shivered when she started noticing the details.

The woman's eyes had been changed. Not with a pinprick, no, this time, they'd been crossed out, with a small X.

The man's eyes had been completely removed, just holes remaining.

To the right of the couple was an old tree. A heart had been carved into it. AJ realized that the space had originally been blank—the giver of the card could draw in whatever initials they wanted.

The sender of this card had put **AJ + ME** in the center of the heart.

"Grammatically speaking, shouldn't that be AJ and I?" Bea said, her voice faint.

AJ appreciated her attempt to lighten the situation. "You're one to talk. Have you ever looked at any of the texts you send?"

She needed to keep moving or she might start shaking too hard with fear. She took several pictures of the day's card and sent them to Officer Brandon. Then she grabbed a plastic baggie from her kitchen and slid both the card and the envelop into it.

"I need to get to work," AJ told Bea as she tucked the card into her purse.

"Oh, no, you do not," Bea said, rounding on her. "You should stay right here."

"What, like a sitting duck? No, thank you. At the inn, I'll be surrounded by people all day. I won't be alone," AJ assured Bea.

"And tonight?" Bea said.

AJ sighed. "I'm going out to dinner with Roland, remember?"

That at least put a teasing smile on Bea's face. "And after that?"

"Chances are, I'll show up at your place again," AJ said. She and Roland had been moving pretty slowly. She didn't want to rush things.

However, she did agree with Bea that being alone tonight might not be her smartest move.

"All right," Bea said, finally mollified. "I'm going to be checking in on you today, though. If I don't get a text back after fifteen minutes—"

"An hour," AJ interjected. "I have meetings today."

"Fine, an hour, I'm calling in the cavalry," Bea said.

"That's acceptable," AJ said. "Though once I'm on my date with Roland, you don't have to worry so much."

"Oh no, sister mine, that's when I'll worry the most. I will want updates! Regularly!" Bea teased.

AJ glared. "Won't you by busy yourself with your husband?"

Bea pressed her lips together tightly at that. "Maybe," she said after a few moments. "Uhm, make sure you give us plenty of warning before you come over. Okay?"

"Believe me, I will," AJ promised. "Because, ewww."

Bea snorted but didn't disagree.

The sisters got back into the car, AJ pausing to look around as they walked. She didn't see anyone nearby. No one was watching them. She also didn't have the feeling of eyes on them.

Bea insisted on dropping AJ off directly in front of the inn, then watching as she made her way into the building.

On the one hand, it was nice that Bea was so worried about her.

On the other hand, AJ needed to get this case solved as soon as possible, because her younger sister was still a brat. Despite them being friends now.

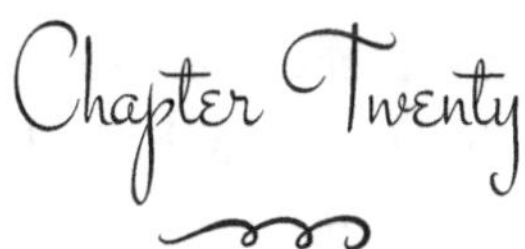

Chapter Twenty

AJ had taken Bea's warnings to heart and she'd tried not to be alone for most of the morning. She'd worked out at reception, checking guests in, supplying extra towels and recommending lunch options for tourists. That afternoon would be even more busy, she was certain.

In between, she occasionally darted back to her office to do things, such as update the website with more events and make sure that payroll had run. She unsuccessfully tried not to feel paranoid about being in her office with no one there.

Not even Gladys came to visit her. She hadn't been around since Monday, when she'd given AJ that vision of Carla. Had she used up so much power she couldn't return? AJ didn't know.

She had the feeling, though, that Gladys's hold on the everyday world was weakening.

AJ would be sad if Gladys left. She gave the inn a certain character. Yet, AJ also hoped that the ghost could rest now that she knew what had happened to her, how she'd been killed.

Just before noon, AJ walked out of her office, down the narrow hallway, to the back door of the kitchen. Payne was rapidly chopping up something red on one of the stainless steel counters. He was still the most handsome man she'd ever met, his head down, the thick black hair just starting to gray. Muscles on his forearms bulged appealingly as he wielded his knife. His skin was still a bronze color of some sort of tanned god. His hands moved unerringly, at a speed that most humans couldn't match.

Then AJ looked down at what he was working on.

Was that a heart?

She gulped and took another step into his domain.

No. It was a beet.

She made herself breathe deeply, telling her own heart to settle down.

She waited until Payne had paused momentarily in between hapless vegetable. "Are we meeting today?" she said softly.

Payne raised his knife as if it were a weapon. He glared at her.

Despite how beautiful Payne was, and how much he did for the inn, AJ still had difficulty trusting him. Particularly when he looked at her with those crazy eyes.

"I suppose. If you insist. But I'm busy here. Meet you out front in," he paused, glancing at the pot beside him, "ten?"

"Sounds good," AJ said, nodding. She walked out of the kitchen and back around to the café. There was still a little coffee in the air pot, which she helped herself to, before starting another pot. The inn generally served coffee all day for free to guests.

Though Rosita and her family, who were now the new owners of the inn, had plans for renovating the café, it was pretty far down on the list of things that needed doing. While the café brought in some business, as well as a lot of locals, the pumps for the bathhouse needed to be replaced first. Payne had actually agreed to that plan as he was the one responsible for cleaning out the filters on a regular basis. New pumps and new filters meant less work for him outside of the kitchen.

The café had last been renovated in the '70s, and not in a chic way. It was all cheap wood paneling, flimsy benches and chairs, tables with old black-and-white postcards stuck under scratched-and-yellowed resin, with a stained linoleum floor.

AJ had seen the plans that Rosita had caused to be drawn up, opening up the area to be more modern, with a dark-red tile floor, much better lights, the tables and chairs replaced with more modern versions. They still had some bench seating, but had replaced them with better models.

AJ had expressed her concern that Rosita's initial plans were a bit too modern. The inn itself was ancient, having opened in 1913. They should hold onto some of the existing character of the place, have a good mix of old and new.

Rosita had listened to her and had talked with the design firm about redoing the plans.

AJ sat with her back to the kitchen, watching the ebb and flow of guests through the reception area, ready to jump in if a line formed.

Fortunately, Payne showed up before she could leave.

"So, I'm assuming you want to talk about tonight's

dinner," Payne said as he sat down heavily in the chair across the table from her. His scowl was particularly impressive, ready to dent concrete if he walked into a wall.

"Do we need to talk about it? You already have that all handled and planned, don't you?" AJ said, curious.

"I, uh, yeah, I do," Payne said. He looked momentarily confused. "What are we meeting about?"

"About next month's event," AJ said.

"Right," Payne said, nodding slowly. They tossed ideas back and forth for a "March Madness" dinner. Not that they were a sports bar. There weren't any TVs in the dining room, and AJ knew that if she suggested putting some in, Payne might actually take a cleaver to them. "Accidentally" of course.

No, what she was proposing was either a feast for the wives while their husbands were consumed by the games, or a carry-out dinner, so that people could eat something other than pizza and chips while watching the games.

Payne liked the thought of the second one, as AJ had suspected he would. It fed into his philosophy that people should eat better than the Standard American Diet, or SAD as he generally called it.

So they came up with a meal plan, something light and simple to heat up. Payne insisted that a large salad be delivered with every meal, which would bring the cost up, but also the healthiness of it.

When they finished their planning, Payne didn't hurry away immediately but sat back in his chair, gazing thoughtfully at AJ.

"Yes?" she said after a few moments.

"It's been okay working with you," Payne said slowly.

"Thanks, I think?" AJ teased.

Payne rolled his eyes at her. "You know. I don't deal well with change."

That raised AJ's eyebrows. She'd known it from day one —it was one of the things that Eva had warned her about.

She hadn't been aware, though that Payne understood how much of a stick in the mud he could be. It was partly why they hadn't emphasized renovating the café, as that would have been too much change all at once for him.

"Are you feeling better about the changes we've made?" AJ asked.

Payne grimaced, then tilted his head from side to side, as if he couldn't make up his mind. "Maybe," he finally admitted. "But that doesn't mean you can just come back in here and tear everything up."

"I hear you," AJ assured the man. She paused, thoughtful.

"I've seen that look before," Payne said. At least he didn't sound too resentful. "You have a non-related question for me. You're curious about something. Or someone."

"True," AJ admitted. "You grew up here. Do you know of anyone named Palmer? Greg Palmer, in particular?"

Payne's glare grew harsh. "Andy Palmer was my dealer," he said shortly.

"Oh," AJ said. "And Greg Palmer..."

"Is Andy's little brother," Payne said. "The family moved away years ago, after Andy overdosed."

"So they don't live here anymore?" AJ asked.

Payne shook his head. "Not that I've heard. I also don't travel in those circles anymore," he pointed out.

"What can you tell me about Greg Palmer?" AJ persisted.

"I can only tell you about when he was a kid," Payne said. "Andy was an asshole. I was an asshole too, though, at the time. You see, Andy kept spiking Greg's orange juice with LSD and other hallucinogenic drugs. Then, he laughed his ass off when Greg started talking about seeing things and hearing voices."

Payne sighed. He looked troubled. "I didn't stop it. I should have at least said something. But I just laughed right along with Andy."

"What happened to Greg?" AJ said.

"I don't know," Payne said. "I did find him, after I'd gotten sober. To apologize for being such an asshole. But he was too far gone. He said we'd put him in touch with the spirit world, and that even without the drugs, the spirits kept talking to him. Telling him to do things."

"Like what?" AJ said, curious. Had the hallucinogenic drugs done something to Greg? Altered his brain such that he was able to communicate with ghosts?

Payne just blew out a loud breath. "Don't know. Didn't want to hear about it. Though I suppose *you* might have a professional interest."

"Greg Palmer was supposedly Carla Lowenstein's boyfriend," AJ said softly.

"The psychic who was killed this weekend?" Payne said.

"Yes," AJ said.

Payne sighed and thought for a moment. "Greg had a thing for what he called 'real' psychics. So many were fakes. He was intent on proving them wrong, showing them to be charlatans. *He* was the real thing. Not them."

"Huh," was all AJ could say.

Greg—GrayDawn—had been certain that Carla was the real thing.

Had there been a confrontation? When he'd demanded that she have a vision or foretell something? Had she failed a crucial test, which was how she ended up drowned?

"Anything else? I need to get back to preparing dinner," Payne said, rising from his chair.

"No, thanks, though," AJ said. "Say, do you think a lot of other people know about Greg Palmer's history?" She didn't add *like the police* though she thought it really loudly.

"Doubt it," Payne said. "Andy's parents were really hands-off. Don't think they'd meant to have kids in the first place. After Andy, then Greg, started getting in trouble, they just kind of disowned them. Walked away."

With that, Payne sauntered back to his domain, the kitchen, leaving AJ stewing on what she'd learned.

It didn't make her feel any better, knowing that there might be a reason why Greg Palmer was after her.

What if she, too, couldn't produce a vision on demand?

Chapter Twenty-One

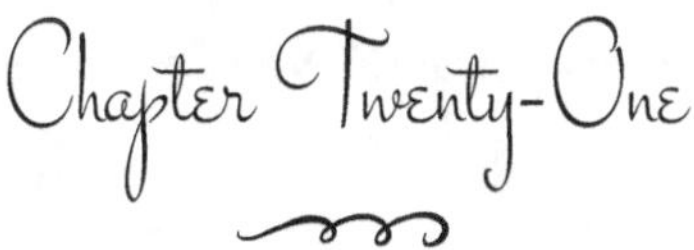

AJ handed Officer Brendan the latest Valentine's Day card that she'd received. Officer Naomi had accompanied him to see her at the inn. Neither of them were trying to be the bad cop that afternoon, which made AJ grateful.

"Were you ever able to find Greg Palmer?" AJ asked.

"Where did you hear that name?" Officer Naomi asked sternly.

"That was Carla's boyfriend, right?" AJ said innocently. "Everyone knows that."

Officer Naomi looked down and pinched the bridge of her nose for a few moments. "Right. Small town. Got it." She looked up, exacerbated at AJ. "Have you had any contact with Greg Palmer?"

"No, but I did learn something about his history today," AJ said. She told them about Andy Palmer drugging his brother, how Greg had visions that he thought were real, how he was obsessed with psychics.

The two police officers looked at each other. AJ

couldn't get a good read off them. Was this new information? Or just confirming things that they already knew?

Possibly a little of both.

"We will certainly keep trying to find Greg Palmer," Officer Brendan assured AJ. "Now, what are your plans for the evening?"

AJ snickered at the shocked look that Officer Naomi threw Officer Brendan. He really needed to learn how to sound more official, so women wouldn't think he was hitting on them. "I think I told you. Roland Jax and I are going out to eat. Then he's dropping me off at my sister's house. I plan on spending the weekend there, and not at my house, except for readings."

"Good, good," Officer Brendan said. He finally seemed to catch on that something might be amiss, as he glanced at Officer Naomi and said, "What?"

"Never mind," Officer Naomi said. She paused, then added, "You be careful."

"I will be," AJ said. She wasn't about to tell them that she'd had a vision about what might happen if she weren't.

When AJ was officially finished with work, she changed out of her office clothes and into her date clothes. She'd agreed with Bea that she needed to up her game some, and had brought in a little black dress. The cut was plain—sleeveless, almost down to her knees, with a scoop neck that didn't show much cleavage (not that AJ had much to show). However, it was made from a material that shimmered as she walked, blues, golds, and greens. It was subtle and one of her favorite new dresses.

She'd applied her makeup in the staff bathroom, and

was back at her desk cleaning things up, when music suddenly blared from her phone.

What was that? Had she accidentally changed her ringtone or something?

She pulled her cellular out of her purse. Evidently, there was a radio app on her phone. Must have been something that came with it because she hadn't downloaded it. It was playing another older song, from the 1960s, something about coming down in three-part harmony.

As AJ looked at the app, trying to figure out how to kill it, the music faded and was replaced with static.

A sibilant whisper hissed under the static. AJ held the phone up to her ear, trying to make out the words.

The temperature in the office abruptly plummeted. Yet, AJ didn't feel a presence, not exactly. Gladys hadn't come to see her.

However, something, or rather, *someone*, was trying to haunt her. Connect with her. Reach her.

What was this person trying to say?

AJ pressed the phone tight against her ear, trying to make out the words.

She would swear that the last word was "me." But was that a separate word, or part of the previous word?

It almost sounded like *salami*, but that didn't make any sense, and the emphasis was wrong. *Sala me*?

Why was a ghost trying to connect with her? Particularly like this?

AJ was embarrassed by how long it took her to finally put the clues together.

She'd been hearing radio music off and on now for the past few days, since Carla's body had been found.

Carla had used a ghost box—an old-fashioned radio—to speak with the spirits.

Maybe now that Carla was a ghost, she was using any nearby radio to try to connect with AJ.

"Carla? Is that you?" AJ asked out loud.

The static was replaced with a squealing noise, like one of those amber alerts. AJ startled, nearly dropping her phone. She quickly discovered that turning down the volume on her phone didn't dim the ear-splitting howl.

As abruptly as the blast had started, it stopped.

AJ's phone went silent.

Heat crept back into her office.

Swell.

She knew, *knew*, that Carla had been trying to reach out to her. Trying to warn her about something.

But what?

And was it already too late for AJ?

Roland texted when he was on his way to the inn to pick AJ up. She'd spent the time trying to re-engage with Carla, but to no avail.

AJ debated turning her phone off so that Carla couldn't disturb her while she was on her date. However, that also meant she wouldn't hear any warnings, either, so AJ left her phone on.

"Looking good!" Sooli called out to AJ as she walked across the lobby to the door.

"Thanks," AJ said. She wasn't the blushing type, but if she had been, this might have been one of those occasions.

Particularly given the grin that the older woman gave her, as well as the enthusiastic thumbs up with both hands.

Though it had been cloudy that morning, it was now clear. Looked as though there could be a nice night for a stroll on the beach. If it wasn't too cold.

Though that might just give couples an excuse to cuddle closer.

Roland drove into the circular drive in front of the inn, parking and hopping out of the car before AJ could let herself in. He'd also dressed up, looking fancier than AJ had yet to see him, wearing a cream-colored shirt, black-and-red striped tie, and a navy suit jacket. He wasn't driving his work truck that night, but his regular little car that looked as though he'd washed it recently.

"You look lovely," Roland assured AJ as he came up to greet her and to hand her a single red rose.

"Thank you," AJ said. "I didn't get you anything." Was she supposed to? It had been so long since she'd dated anyone who was, well, considerate. Ken had never wanted to celebrate any holiday, claiming to be above all those materialistic things.

She wondered if he'd just been that cheap, or maybe he'd been buying presents for the women he been cheating on AJ with, and never getting her anything.

"That's okay," Roland said with a grin. "Your charming company is all I'm going to need tonight."

AJ smiled at him and allowed him to open the car door for her, sliding in. Yup. Roland had gone all out, getting both the inside and the outside of the car detailed. She could smell the cleaner still, a little lemony and sweet.

"Tell me what you're researching," AJ said as a way to

get the conversation ball rolling. Plus, she wasn't quite ready to talk about her week. Not yet.

"There's this new book that's come out about the pirates that plied the west coast," Roland said enthusiastically. "They aren't Disney pirates, but the real deal. Pretty bloodthirsty, preying on smaller boats and cargo ships. Terrorizing sailors and fishermen."

"Is it something I might want to read when you're finished?" AJ asked.

"Naw. It's someone's doctoral thesis that they've expanded for publication. I'll tell you the exciting bits so you don't have to read about all the politics and economic issues," Roland told her.

AJ grinned. While she was interested in history, she didn't have a passion for it like Roland did. Working her way through a thick textbook like that was a sure cure for insomnia, at least for her.

"How about you? How are you holding up?" Roland asked.

AJ couldn't help but sigh. "Things have gotten kind of weird," she admitted. "I asked you about the Valentine's Day cards already, right?"

"Yes," he said, nodding. "Again, going to assume there's nothing to be jealous about, not unless you tell me so."

"No, no need," AJ said. "It turns out that the cards weren't as innocent as they seemed. There were pinpricks in the eyes of the characters. I didn't notice them because they were so small."

"That doesn't sound good," Roland said slowly.

She told him about the last few cards and the messages

on them, assuring him that she'd already been to the police about them.

"So," Roland said after she finished up. "I don't want you to take this the wrong way, but I don't want you to spend the night alone. I can go sleep on the couch if you want to come crash at my place."

"Thank you," AJ said, touched that he was trying to look after her. "But after dinner, I'll have you drop me off at my sister's house."

"And you'll spend the weekend there?" Roland asked, still concerned.

"I will," AJ promised. "I have a few clients coming in on the weekend for readings, but I won't be alone."

"Good," Roland said. "Have you had any visions about something bad happening?"

AJ sighed. This was where it was going to get sticky, she just knew it.

"Yeah, I have," she admitted. She told him about the vision of her house and the lightning.

"Wait, didn't you see that same sort of dark cloud attacking Carla's radio?" Roland asked.

"I did," AJ said. "And I've learned that Carla's supposed boyfriend, Greg Palmer, has a thing about proving that psychics are fakes."

She explained all about Greg Palmer, his background, and how he was probably GrayDawn as well.

"You know, we don't have to stop after we go to dinner," Roland offered. "We could just keep going up the coast. Drive over to Seattle or someplace safer."

"I'll be fine," AJ assured him, still touched. "The vision

was just symbolic, not an actual image of me. I'm sure that I can get out of this alive."

"If you die on my watch, I expect to be haunted thoroughly," Roland said gravely.

"Deal," AJ said. "But speaking of hauntings, I think Carla is now haunting me."

"Really?" Roland asked. He didn't even bother to hide his eagerness.

AJ couldn't help but roll her eyes. "There's no reason for you to be so excited about that."

"It's a ghost! Maybe she has connections to other ghosts," Roland said. "There's so much we can learn!"

"Whatever," AJ said. "If my phone suddenly starts blaring or playing music, you'll know it's her."

"Cool," Roland said, nodding. "Have you been able to talk with her?"

"No, not really. I think she was trying to use the radio app on my phone to communicate with me." She continued, explaining about the ghost box, and how it had been stolen from Carla's office.

"Huh. So radios are her thing?" Roland said. "I've heard stories about that before."

AJ shrugged. "I don't know. Maybe I am just going nuts."

"No, I don't think so," Roland said, turning serious. "I do think that you're under a lot of stress. But even you've told me that you're under less stress now than you had been, when you'd been working in Seattle."

"True," AJ said. "I don't want to say that I've retired, because I haven't. I'm still working. However, the work is so different now. Sometimes, particularly when doing readings and things, it doesn't feel like work."

"Good," Roland said. "I feel that way sometimes when I finish a new landscape project. Sure, it was a lot of work getting it all done. But I feel so satisfied once the project is finished, seeing how good it looks."

"And if someone would just pay you to do historic research..." AJ teased.

"Exactly," Roland said. "I need to find me a good sugar daddy. Or a good sugar momma," he said, throwing a grin her way.

"Sorry," AJ said. "Don't see a lot of money rolling my way." Particularly not as she worked less and less at the inn and was going to have to support herself completely with her psychic business.

"Did you ever have a corporate job? Something that took care of you?" AJ said. "It's one of the things that makes me nervous, sometimes. Going to work for myself."

Roland nodded. "It's a leap of faith," he said seriously. "I certainly had doubts when I started my own business. What would happen if I got sick? Or worse, injured? And I couldn't work anymore? There really wasn't a safety net for me."

AJ didn't say anything, didn't ask about his parents. While she was certain that if something had gone dreadfully wrong that they would have stepped up to help him. On the other hand, the price for that aid would have been exorbitant, at least in emotional costs.

"But to answer your question, no, I never had a 'real' job, as it were," Roland continued. "I finished college and came home, looking for employment. There just wasn't anything. I didn't have a PhD, so I couldn't teach. And teachers make practically nothing in terms of pay. I just couldn't make the numbers work. So I started doing some lawn work on the side, as I'd always loved plants and working outdoors, particularly in the summertime. The clients poured in that summer. When fall came, and I still didn't have a job, I just kept doing lawn work and gardening."

"So it was a gradual thing, going into business on your own," AJ said slowly.

"It was," Roland said. "Kind of like what you're doing. You're still working at the inn, while at the same time, ramping up the psychic business on the side."

"Yeah," AJ said, nodding. She paused, thinking.

At some point, she was going to have to tell Roland about the water magic. It wasn't an easy topic to bring up. *Say, in addition to talking with ghosts and having visions, I can also magically throw water around!*

Maybe she would try to tell him later that night. If it came up. Somehow.

In the meanwhile, she was going to enjoy this slice of normality.

For however long it lasted.

Chapter Twenty-Two

The restaurant—Coastal Meats—didn't look like much. It was off the main highway, up a winding slope, surrounded by pines. They appeared to be at a small cabin. The walls were made from wooden logs, and there was an actual rack of antlers attached to a board just above the door. The parking lot itself was a little dark, with the building being the only oasis of light in the area.

"Are we there yet?" AJ teased when Roland parked the car.

Roland merely rolled his eyes at her. "It's actually a bigger building than it seems. The front is kind of small, but the building goes back quite a ways. There are banquet rooms and everything."

When they stepped out into the quiet night she heard the rushing of water in the distance. "Is there a river nearby?"

"Yeah, just down the hill. Out behind the restaurant is a large green space. In the summer, they cater parties there."

The wind had picked up while they'd been driving. AJ felt the rain in the air, a promise of more water soon.

Roland offered AJ his arm and she tucked her hand into his elbow. He certainly smelled nice, kind of woodsy and masculine, not that obnoxiously sweet body spray that so many of the younger men wore these days. She had a good raincoat on over her dress, something to keep the mist away.

The maître d' was a short man, balding on top with a perfectly trimmed gray and black mustache and goatee. He gave them a warm smile when they entered, taking them back to their table right away.

The wooden walls of the main dining room were golden, making the room feel more cozy. At least twenty small tables were scattered across the floor, with large booths seating six to eight along two sides of the room. A bar took up the far wall, with three shelves of all the fanciest bottles of alcohol that you could ask for.

It looked more like a high-end steakhouse than a fancy, fine-dining restaurant. However, glancing around, AJ saw that everyone was dressed up, the men in suits and ties, the women all in dresses.

The maître d' rolled AJ's chair back for her. It was covered in black, brass-studded leather, with a rounded back and arms on the sides. It was surprisingly comfortable once AJ settled herself. They weren't appropriate for the inn, but she still thought about them for a moment.

Before handing them heavy menus encased in leather folders, the maître d' unfolded the heavy white linen napkin tented up on the table and handed it to AJ, then did the same for Roland.

"Bon Appetit!" he said as he poured them water from

the bottle already on their table. "If you need anything special, don't hesitate to ask."

AJ leaned across the table after the maître d' had left. "Wow," she said softly. "I had no idea how upscale this place was."

Roland just grinned at her. "It doesn't look that fancy from the outside. But I know it's special. My parents are regulars here."

AJ just nodded, particularly after glancing at the prices. Wow. Roland really had come from money if his parents ate at this place often. For her, it was going to be a once-a-year occasion, and only if she was having a particularly good year.

"We're splitting the check, right?" AJ said when she glanced back up.

Roland seemed a little surprised. "We can, but we don't have to. I'm happy to take you out, foot the bill."

"But it's a lot," AJ said. Even the appetizers were pricier than what she was comfortable with.

"Too much?" Roland asked. "We can go someplace else, if you want."

AJ sighed. "No, we'll eat here. But I am paying for half of it." Otherwise, it was just too much to ask, particularly as this was their first date.

"Okay," Roland said, obviously prepared to roll with the punches.

They finally decided to order the special, a complete five-course meal for two. The price was actually better than ordering things separately.

They got to choose options for most of the courses, and

they agreed to get different things so they could try and taste everything.

For the first course, AJ got the lime-and-mescal ceviche, while Roland got the shrimp cocktail. They were both divine. The cocktail sauce wasn't the usual ketchup mixed with horseradish, no, someone had made it from scratch, and added something that gave it a lovely smoky flavor. AJ's ceviche was refreshing and tasty, also with a bit of smoke (probably from the mescal).

Once those plates were cleared away, the servers brought them each two small wafers. They looked like what AJ had been served at communion, that one time she'd gone to church with a friend.

The wafers were flavored with the slightest hint of lemon and melted on her tongue. Only after she was finished did she realize that these were palate cleansers, meant to help wash away the taste of the previous course and get them ready for the next one.

"I'm glad I wore a loose dress," AJ joked. "Because I'm going to stuff myself here, if the rest of the courses are as good as that first one."

Roland looked down at his belly and groaned. "I didn't. I wonder what they'd think if I changed into sweats midway through the meal."

AJ shrugged. "I wouldn't hold it against you. This has already been fabulous. Thank you."

Roland grinned at her. "They don't serve huge portions, despite the prices," he assured her. "I'm happy we're trying the special though. Tonight should be special."

"Our first date, huh?" AJ teased.

"Exactly," Roland said.

"Tell me about the worst meal you've ever had," AJ said after a moment.

"Just to make this one more special? Okay," Roland thought for a moment. "I was dating a woman who was vegetarian, though she flirted with vegan too. I decided to make us pizza one night."

AJ nodded, grinning. Roland had already admitted that while he liked eating out at fancy places, he wasn't much of a cook.

"The dough was pretty easy, actually. But I didn't have any tomato paste for the sauce. So I took ketchup and just added some oregano to it."

AJ snorted. Even she knew that wasn't a good idea.

"I layered bits of green and red peppers, along with spinach and some tofu. Then, I tried using vegan cheese. Did you know that stuff doesn't melt?" Roland said. "It just laid there and glistened, coated in oil, like it was actually made of plastic or something. All the vegetables were black on the edges and that stupid cheese never melted. The dough also burned. She still insisted that we eat it, because I'd gone to all the effort to make it." He sighed and shook his head. "We should have thrown it out and ordered something."

AJ shook her head. "One of my worst meals was when my mom decided that she was going to 'educate' my palate. She started serving me weird things, like paté, blue cheese, and snails."

"How old were you?" Roland said.

"Eight, I think. It went over about as well as you might imagine," AJ said. She shook her head. She would never forget the look on her mom's face when AJ, her good, pliable, reliable daughter, finally threw her plate onto the floor, begging her mom for some real food.

The salad course arrived next. They hadn't had a choice with this, and each got the same salad. The bed of romaine lettuce was decorated with nuggets of goat cheese, small pieces of pickled red and golden beets, spicy pumpkin seeds, and a delicious lemon-poppyseed dressing.

"Salad shouldn't taste this good," Roland said. He sounded suspicious of it.

"What, do you think there's a witch in the kitchen, casting spells on the food so that the guests will find it amazing?" AJ said lightly.

She knew she was looking for an opening, to see how Roland felt about actual magic, beyond the ghosts and the visions.

Roland merely grinned at her. "No, it's probably just tattooed psychopaths with knives back there," he said. "It's an ordinary magic."

AJ nodded. "Do you believe in extraordinary magic?" she asked seriously, not meeting his eye.

The expressive sigh he gave surprised her, and she looked up.

"Ghosts are one thing," Roland said seriously. "Too many people have experienced Gladys for me to deny it. In addition, more than a few weird occurrences have happened on the ghost walk for me to really deny it."

AJ could tell he wasn't finished, so sat quietly waiting as he took another bite of the truly amazing salad.

"I know you have visions," Roland continued softly. "If it was anyone else telling me that they saw things in a bowl of water, I wouldn't believe them."

"So other people don't have magic?" AJ said, unsure of how she felt about his answer.

"You tell me," Roland said. "Do other people have power like yours?"

"You're aware that Ursula did, right?" AJ said.

Roland shrugged. "Never saw it. Though I know plenty of people in town who swear she was the real deal. Like Eva."

AJ nodded, remembering how the former owner of the inn had dragged her to Ursula's house. "According to Ursula, it's pretty rare," she admitted. After a few moments, she added, "There's a chance that Carla might have had some magic."

"Really?" Roland said. "You always maintained that she was a con artist."

"Yeah, and I'm still not sure she had any divination skills. However, she might have been able to connect with ghosts." That would certainly explain AJ's vision about seeing where Carla's body was.

They didn't say anything for a few moments as the servers cleared away the dishes, handing them more of the wafers. This time, instead of being lemony, they were tangier, more like grapefruit.

"Honestly, I'm not sure how I feel about Carla possibly having magic, a solid connection to ghosts," Roland said.

"But you're always wanting to talk with ghosts," AJ said.

"Yeah, but I'm a nobody. Not a potential practioner," Roland said. "I don't know. It's a lot to take in, you know? That the world might not be how I've always experienced it? That there might be a whole lot more?"

AJ nodded. "If it helps, Bea sometimes has issues with it as well. And she's known me her entire life."

Roland gave her a solid smile. "It does, actually. Was Bea surprised by your powers?"

"No," AJ said, still slightly miffed by that. "She claims I was always weird."

Soup was served before they could say much more. Roland had ordered the cream of tomato, while AJ had the butternut squash. Both soups were amazing, and though AJ was already feeling full, she didn't bother stopping until her bowl was empty.

"So Bea isn't surprised by you becoming a psychic?" Roland said, returning the conversation to that.

"Not really," AJ said. She told him about answering the phone before it rang when she was a kid.

"Huh," was Roland's only response.

AJ knew she had to change the topic. "What was one of the favorite things you got to do as a kid?"

Roland easily let go of the previous topic and regaled her with stories about his past. It was obvious that he'd found the good parts and held onto them, instead of being bitter about how his parents had treated him.

Those stories took them through the main course as well. It was a surf-and-turf dinner, with lobster tail and steak, colorful fingerling potatoes that had been cooked in garlic and rosemary, and a few artfully arranged stems of steamed broccolini.

After the first bite of the lobster, AJ realized she'd never had really well cooked lobster before. The texture was soft and creamy, better than she'd ever tasted. The herbed butter that it was served with was flavorful, yet at the same time, didn't overpower the lobster.

"I'm never going to have lobster ever again at any other restaurant," AJ said.

"I know, right?" Roland said with a grin.

They had just finished eating that course, and had sat back, stuffed but happy. The steaks had also been perfectly cooked and rested. Not quite tender enough to cut with a spoon, though verging on it.

"And there's still dessert to come," Roland warned AJ.

She just groaned in return. She'd be happy to sit there and digest for the next week, like some kind of predator who'd just eaten an entire herd of cattle.

Then her phone started blaring.

Chapter Twenty-Three

AJ tried, but couldn't get her phone to shut up. Turning the volume down didn't do any good.

Other people in the restaurant were now looking at them.

"Sorry. I'll be right back," AJ promised as she hurried away from the table.

She walked back toward the restrooms, hoping that the noise might be less disturbing back there. However, there was a mother nursing a baby in the front part of the incredibly posh space. AJ turned right around and kept looking for someplace quieter.

At least the blaring went away and the static came back. There were words again. AJ couldn't hear them over the music the roar of conversations. Roland had mentioned that there were banquet rooms, and at least one of them appeared full at the moment.

Hurrying down the hallway, past a door that led to a chaotic (and loud) kitchen, she reached a door leading outside, with the exit sign above it clearly marked.

As soon as AJ stepped outside she found herself taking a deep breath. She hadn't realized how tense she'd gotten with her phone misbehaving as it had been.

She could finally hear the words as well. Or most of them.

Was the person saying, "Follow me"? or "Don't follow me"? AJ couldn't tell for certain. Or if the person was saying both phrases, and switching from one to the other.

She pressed the phone up tightly to her ear, only to be rewarded with another loud squealing alarm.

"Dang it!" AJ said, holding the phone at arm's length, glaring at it.

A chill passed through her. The rain she'd smelled on the air earlier had arrived, though just a light mist at this time. She could see her breath when she huffed.

Or was it just that cold where she was standing? Had a ghost come to visit?

"What do you want? Why are you bothering me?" AJ fumed.

The static returned with the whispered words. Maybe it was "Don't follow me."

But where? Where did the ghost *not* want her to go?

The words petered out. AJ growled in frustration. This wasn't helping, wasn't actually getting her anywhere.

She turned to go back into the restaurant.

A man stood between her and the building. She hadn't heard him come up. Then again, she'd only been listening to her phone.

He was thin, as if put together with sticks. His hair was an unnatural light gray color, like the pelt of an elephant plushy. Blue streaks decorated his bangs. Even in the dim light shining over the door to the restaurant, AJ had the impression of wide, staring eyes and a dark frown. His hoodie was a lighter gray than his hair, and his jeans were black.

"Greg Palmer?" AJ said.

The man glanced around the parking lot quickly.

No one else was back here. No one else was around.

They were all alone.

"You still see too much," he said. He took what looked like a gray scanner out of his pocket, the kind that clerks used in stores to scan prices.

Buzzing lines of lightning blazed from the device, striking AJ. Electricity coursed through her, shocking her. Her last regret was that she hadn't got to have the last course of her dinner—an incredibly decadent chocolate and caramel mousse—then dark waves crashed over her, taking her down.

AJ woke trying to jerk head back, to get away from whatever foul stench had appeared just under her nose.

She couldn't get very far, though.

Trying to raise a hand to ward off whatever that awful smell was brought home the fact that she couldn't move her arms. She was tied down, her hands behind her, sitting in a chair, her legs bound as well.

Crap.

AJ shook her head, the fear spiking through her bringing her all the way to wakefulness.

Or nightmarehood. Take your pick.

She was tied to a chair in what looked like a basement. Had Greg carried her there? He must be a lot stronger than he looked. The floor beneath her was dirt. Smells of mold and slowly rotting wood filled the air. She looked up, past Greg Palmer, who was still standing in front of her, and around the room.

The cinderblock walls held skinny windows at head height, still showing the darkness of the night outside. A workbench stood to her left, the loops and hooks for tools all empty. Rusting metal garbage bins full of pieces of wood sat in front of it. A long fluorescent light hung over the space, adding a faint buzz to the cool air.

The wall in front of her as well as to the right held shelves that were mostly empty. An occasional can of food still graced the space, though the labels were long gone. When AJ turned further, she found the stairs going back up.

Her escape.

Somehow.

She turned back to Greg. He'd stepped to the side and revealed something she hadn't noticed before: a table pushed up against the wall, with Carla's ghost box sitting in the middle of it. A lamp had been clamped to the table, its light directed at the radio.

Greg noticed that AJ had finally seen the ghost box. "Can you make it work?" he said.

He sounded eager.

AJ shook her head, though she regretted the movement. Everything muscle and joint hurt from the taser. "No, I can't. You know that I can't. That was Carla's box. It was *her* way of interacting with the spirits."

Greg Palmer growled, low and deep in his throat. He

turned and glared at AJ. She tried to stop herself from flinching at his rage.

Why was he so angry? Was it because she'd dared to talk about Carla?

"Why did you steal Carla's ghost box?" AJ asked. Figured that she might as well ask.

"It was mine, not hers," Greg said. "I made it."

"Really? You made that yourself?" AJ felt as though she had to ask.

"All right, so I originally made it for her," Greg admitted. "But she was teaching me how to use it. How to cast the voices everywhere, like she did."

"What do you mean?" AJ said, her curiosity almost overcoming her fear.

Almost.

"She would start up the ghost box, and at first, all the voices she talked to just came out of it. But then, they would start speaking from other parts of the room," Greg explained. "I'd thought she'd put in hidden speakers or something. I even drilled into the walls. But there weren't any speakers. The voices all came from her."

The amount of wonder in his voice surprised AJ, particularly given how torn apart Carla's office had been. "So that was you," she said. It made sense, now, given how she'd thought the scene showed someone searching frantically for something.

Looking, and not finding.

"The ghost box was mine," Greg said, raising his chin defiantly. "Carla would have wanted me to have it."

"Why did you kill her?" AJ said. "If the voices were coming from her?"

"I didn't mean to!" Greg protested strongly.

AJ didn't respond. What, he hadn't meant to wrap that boat anchor around her legs so her body wouldn't float up? How did that work, exactly?

"She'd told me she had a bad heart," Greg said. "I just—I didn't believe her. Or remember. Until afterward. When I hit her with the taser, she went down. And stayed down. I kept trying to wake her back up, but she wouldn't. So I had to hide the body."

"Oh," AJ said. So it really had been an accident. "Good thing I have a strong heart then, eh?"

Greg shrugged. "Wouldn't have minded you getting it. You're a fake."

AJ shook her head. "No, I'm not, and you know it."

Why else had he been "gifting" her with Valentine's Day cards, with the eyes poked out, if not to blind her? Because he was afraid of what she saw?

Greg just glared at her again. "But you can't make the ghost box work. Or teach me how to make it work."

AJ remembered her conversation with Willow, about how she couldn't be her teacher, as their magic was so different. "No, I can't," she said. "That isn't how I reach the spirits. Or do magic."

If she could only get him to bring her some water. That would make all the difference in the world.

"I contact the spirits through water," AJ said. "A bowl filled with water."

"I heard about that," Greg said, scowling.

"If you bring me a bowl with water in it, I'll show you," AJ said. "I can teach you how to reach the spirits that way."

It didn't matter that she was lying. She didn't know if

Greg could reach any spirits that way. All she really needed was some water.

Greg considered it, his wild eyes looking at her, then darting to the corners of the room behind her.

AJ made herself sit still, telling herself that there really wasn't anything behind her. It was just Greg being freaked out, possibly high on something.

Did he have any power? Could he talk with ghosts? Or had it all been Carla?

"All right," Greg said after a few moments. "I'll give you a chance to prove yourself."

He walked away from her. She heard him stomping up the stairs.

AJ quickly started tugging at her bonds. There was no give. She glanced down, looking at her legs. Zip ties were wrapped around her ankles, giving her very little room to move. It was probably why she could barely wiggle her arms, as similar zip ties bound her wrists together.

She rocked side to side. Sure, she could fall over, land on the ground. But then what? Where could she go? What could she do? There wasn't a handy knife anywhere, or even a sharp edge that she saw. The pieces of wood in the metal bins didn't have any convenient nails sticking out of them even if she did manage to maneuver herself over there.

At least she spotted her phone, sitting on the table beside the ghost box. She was a little surprised that Carla hadn't tried contacting her again.

Or did the ghost have what she wanted? Had she wanted AJ to go and confront Greg?

To follow her into death?

Follow me, don't follow me?

Before AJ could form any additional impossible plans, Greg came tromping down the stairs again. He carried a filthy green-plastic bowl over to the table and set it down. Then he flicked open a red box cutter and came toward AJ.

She couldn't help but shrink back. He gave her a knowing smirk, but all he did was to cut off the zip ties binding her. She stayed seated, rubbing her wrists and her hands while he knelt down to do her legs.

If this was an action movie, she'd be able to somehow kick him across the room as soon as he'd freed one leg. But AJ could only groan in appreciation for the blood to start flowing into her feet, the tingling bite of pins and needles distracting all thoughts of escape.

As soon as AJ was free Greg backed away, the taser now in his hand, pointing directly at her. "I won't hesitate to use this," he warned her. "Since your heart can take it," he added with a sly grin.

"Thanks for the warning," AJ said. She lurched to her feet. Dang it! That hurt. Her toes cried out in pain, but AJ stubbornly walked forward to the welcome bowl of water.

For a moment, she had the urge to stick her full head in it. She settled for dipping her hands in the surprisingly cold water. Despite the dirt still clinging to the rim of the bowl, the water smelled fresh.

"Rainwater?" she asked, looking back over her shoulder at Greg. He had removed himself, and was standing next to the abandoned workbench, several feet away.

What was the range on that taser? Five feet? Ten feet? And how much had he amped the voltage in it to knock her completely out?

"Yeah, it's rainwater," he said, nodding slowly. "It's really coming down out there."

AJ spent a moment studying him. He hadn't gone too far from the house, as his gray hoodie was still mostly dry.

"You know there's more to this world than just connecting with ghosts, or seeing the future, right?" AJ asked as she turned back to the bowl of water.

It had no shimmer to it, no alluring light warning of an incoming vision. Instead, the water had quickly grown muddied from the dirt encrusting the bowl.

AJ scooped out a handful of water, then lifted it up, letting the water slowly dribble out of her palm, back into the bowl.

She slowed the fall of the water, until it was a very thin stream running from her hand to the bowl.

Then she took her hand away.

The small pocket of water that she'd held in her palm remained in the air, connected by a needle thin stream to the bowl.

"Wait. How did you do that?" Greg asked, taking a step closer.

AJ just nodded to him as the water splashed down in the bowl. She could only hold the water up like that for a short while.

And she needed Greg to get closer, so she could really wallop him with a fist of water magic.

"See?" AJ said. She reached down and drew the water up between her fingers, as if it was some sort of clay. "There are many things that can be done."

Greg shook his head, blinking, squeezing his eyes shut

for a few moments before opening them again. "You're trying to trick me," he accused her.

"I'm not," AJ said softly. "I'm the real deal, at least when it comes to magic."

She'd never showed anyone her magic, not really. Bea only got the aftereffects of her drying spells. And her sister had never wanted to see more.

If AJ got away, she figured that no one would pay attention to Greg's rantings about her manipulating the water.

It was a risk, but one she felt she had to take.

"You also have visions in the water?" Greg said, sounding hopeful at last.

"I do. Not from the radio, not like Carla," AJ said.

She wasn't sure if that was a mistake or not, to remind him of his former girlfriend, the one who'd finally figured out that Greg was all kinds of crazy.

"Carla couldn't do that to the water, not like you can," Greg said. He stayed where he was.

Could AJ just throw the entire bowl at him? And not get hit with the taser?

"Could she manipulate the air, though? Make it colder or hotter, or cause breezes to occur?" AJ asked.

Greg looked thoughtful for a moment. "Maybe," he said. "I was never sure if she was faking it or not."

AJ merely nodded. "There are different powers," she said. "What is your power, Greg?"

He smiled for a moment, hefting the taser up. "Electricity," he said firmly. "And I want you to show me how to make the lightning flash from my fingers."

AJ blinked, surprised. "I don't know how to do that. I'm not sure anyone does," she said. Though why stop at just fire, earth, air and water? Maybe there were some electric powers as well.

"My main element is water, Greg," AJ told him firmly. "Like this." She drew up peak after peak of water, like molding frosting on a cake, drawing the tips up just above the top of the bowl and holding them there.

Greg took another step toward her, halving the distance. He was on the outside of her range, given the amount of liquid she had to work with.

It would have to do.

"Greg, have you ever considered what you're doing?" AJ said. She purposefully dropped her voice to a mere whisper by the end of the sentence.

It worked. It got him to lean in, putting his face closer to her.

"What did you say?"

AJ abruptly scooped out a handful of water and threw it at Greg. He reared back as the fist formed as well as dodged to the side.

The water-fist gave him a glancing blow and he tottered to one side.

Most importantly, he dropped the taser.

AJ didn't bother scrambling for it. Instead, she raced up the stairs, blowing through the door and into what appeared to be an abandoned house.

No wonder the cops hadn't been able to find Greg. He'd been camping out here.

She had the briefest impression of busted up furniture, a lighted tent set up in the corner, rain coming down the walls from the leaking roof.

Then she was through the next door, called outside by the water pouring down there.

She'd heard Greg right behind her. She didn't try to run further away.

Instead, she stopped. Turned to face him.

Finally, she had enough water to work with. She instinctively raised up a shield with one hand, while she held out the other, gathering up more rainwater.

Greg came to a stop a few feet away. Even in the dim light she could see his smirk.

Did he honestly believe she was helpless here, with the glorious water around her?

He raised his taser and shot it.

AJ flinched as the bright lines of electricity darted out.

However, they couldn't pass through her shield.

Instead, they bounced off.

And with a little guidance, ended up impaling Greg's chest.

Chapter Twenty-Four

Though Officer Brendan gave AJ some questioning looks, Officer Naomi was more than happy to believe AJ's account, that she'd tricked Greg into giving her a bowl of water, flung it at him to distract him, had grabbed his taser when he'd dropped it, then used it on him after they'd gotten outside.

All that talk of her doing magic with the water? That was just her trying to get away. Lying to her captor. He knew that she was a psychic. Easy enough to take it one step further.

(Much later that year, Greg was found criminally insane. AJ figured that his continued claims that she had magic probably hadn't helped in terms of the diagnosis. The state had institutionalized him. Though AJ felt some relief at the news, she also hoped that he was now getting the medication and therapy he needed.)

AJ hadn't dared use her drying spell after the cops had picked her up. So she sat, wet and miserable through their questioning at the police station.

As soon as she could, AJ texted Roland to let him know that she was safe and that she'd explain everything later. Then she called Bea, who rushed over to pick her up at the police station.

AJ raced out to the car as soon as Bea pulled up, sliding into the warmth, then pausing for a moment to finally dry herself off thoroughly.

Bea glared at her from the driver's seat. "Are you finished?"

AJ shivered. "I am," she said meekly.

It was only then that she noticed that Bea was wearing her bathrobe and not much else.

"Uhm, sorry for disturbing you?" AJ said.

Bea waved a dismissive hand. "Yeah. It's okay. Picking up my sister from the police station was an interruption that Peter was willing to tolerate. What happened to you? And your date?"

AJ quickly summed up her evening as they drove back to Bea's place.

"I can get my things and go, so you'll have the rest of the night alone," AJ offered.

"Oh, no you are not," Bea said. "I'm sitting you down and pouring half a bottle of wine into you. Maybe a sleeping pill as well. Then you're spending the weekend relaxing and not worrying about anything."

"I have clients to see on Saturday," AJ said meekly.

That earned her another glare. "Fine. I'll come with you. I know, I know, you caught the bad guy. But give yourself some time to recover. Please? For me?"

AJ nodded, secretly relieved. She was both wired and completely exhausted from the events of the evening.

The weekend passed by in a blur. Bea was true to her word and kept AJ pumped full of wine for much of the time, taking the edge off. She canceled all her clients, and spent the weekend at her sister's vacation rental, pleasantly buzzed.

It kept her from thinking too much, about what Greg might have done to her, about Carla, about everything.

Had Carla been warning her against Greg? *Don't follow me?*

Or had the ghost wanted her to die? *Follow me?*

AJ wasn't sure. All she knew was that she didn't think she could trust Carla the ghost, not like she did Gladys.

By Monday, AJ was finally ready to face the world again. Bea drove her first to her house, to make sure that everything was still fine with it, before AJ took off for work at the inn.

The Milltown app had been full of news about the arrest of GrayDawn, AKA Greg Palmer, and that he'd confessed to the murder of Carla Lowenstein. AJ found herself relieved that the official reports didn't mention her role in his arrest.

Monday morning went by quickly, AJ helping Willow check guests out as well as doing paperwork. No one approached her GrayDawn which made her oh so grateful.

It wasn't until she went to lunch at the Storm Brew Café that anyone even mentioned it.

Of course, it was Fred.

AJ found him sitting in the window seat of the café, busily scribbling in his notebook. He looked the same as always, balding and geeky. He waved to her as she walked by the café, so after AJ ordered her lunch (a vegetable panini—

Bea would be so proud) she walked into the side room at the café.

Fred quickly put aside his notebook as she walked up with her sandwich, waving her to come and sit beside him.

"I heard you had quite the adventure this weekend," he started off with. "What can my muse tell me today?"

AJ nearly rolled her eyes at him. "Don't allow disturbed young men who think they have some sort of gift into your life?"

More details had come out about Greg and Carla, through more anonymous accounts that AJ was certain Fred was behind.

They'd been seeing one another in Portland, but Greg had gotten weird, and Carla had been afraid. So she came to Milltown to start over. Greg had sworn that was the one place he'd never return to, so she thought she was safe there.

She wasn't.

The ghost box remained in police custody. AJ certainly didn't want it. Carla did have relatives somewhere who would eventually take all her belongings.

"Is he really crazy?" Fred inquired, trying for innocence. "Or are his accusations of you accurate?"

AJ narrowed her eyes. Where was Fred getting his information from? He must have a source at the police department.

"You heard about his background, right? Being fed drugs as a young kid?" AJ countered with.

"I did," Fred said. He sounded sad. "Such a waste."

"Exactly," AJ said. She paused, trying to get the conversation going another direction. "How's the next book coming along?"

"Oh!" Fred exclaimed. "It's been fabulous! I just—I keep having all these ideas. Not just for this book, but for others as well."

"That's awesome," AJ told him sincerely. "What's the second book about?"

"The amazingly debonair town gossip is accused of murder. He didn't do it, but he can't break a confidence in order to clear his name. It's been quite a puzzle for the main character, the psychic, to figure out who the actual killer is, in order to protect her dear friend," Fred said with a sly grin.

"That sounds wonderful," AJ told him. "You'll have to let me read these someday."

Fred nodded earnestly. "I will. The first one is with a copyeditor friend of mine right now."

"Really?" AJ asked, surprised. She would have thought that Fred would have rewritten the novel a few times before sending it off, particularly given his previous track record.

Fred leaned forward, lowering his voice. "I have a dear friend who insisted on reading it, even in a draft state. He wouldn't give me any comments, just kept encouraging me to go on. When I finished, he took the book from me and sent it to the copyeditor. He said it was perfect and that she'd catch and fix anything that needed fixing."

Fred possibly looked a little panicked at that.

"Then what will you do after the copyeditor finishes?" AJ asked.

"My friend said I couldn't edit it again after that. That it had to go on and be published," Fred said quietly. "There are so many new tools now, and new technologies. I can publish the book myself, with my friend's help. He already had been in contact with a cover designer."

"That's exciting," AJ said, encouraging him.

"It is," Fred said, though he looked worried. "What if no one buys it, though? Or worse, if everyone does?"

AJ didn't even know how to respond to that. "Your friend will help you through it."

Fred gave a deep sigh. "You're right. He will. I'd love to introduce him to you at some point. But he's...He's very reclusive."

AJ just nodded. She'd always suspected that Fred might prefer men to women, but no one actually knew, and it wasn't something that AJ felt comfortable asking about.

"It's okay," AJ said. "I'm just glad you're doing something with your book."

Fred nodded. "Yes. The first book is done. The second book is started. And now I have yet *another* idea for the third, thanks to you." He gave her a mock glare.

"You're welcome," AJ said.

"And..." Fred added, pausing for a moment before he continued, "if there is something to Greg Palmer's claims, anything at all that you'd like to tell me about, know that I'd keep your secrets in the strictest of confidences."

"I have nothing to confess," AJ said firmly.

Fred gave her a speculative look, but didn't push it.

After lunch, AJ went straight back into her office to do more work.

The room was cold, the temperature hovering at sixty, when she walked in.

"Gladys?" AJ said as she closed the door. At least she hoped it was that ghost. Besides, wouldn't Carla had blared something on her phone?

A presence wafted over AJ and she knew she was no longer alone in the space.

"What is it?"

Desk.

AJ wasn't sure exactly what Gladys wanted, and the word had been whisper-thin.

Still, she put her purse down and walked over to her desk. Without being asked, she pulled out her scrying bowl and poured water into it.

However, after she sat down she didn't feel anything tugging at her. Gladys didn't put her hands on AJ's shoulders, pushing her down and into a vision.

Instead, it felt as though all of Gladys's attention was focused on the bowl of water sitting on AJ's desk.

Frost rimmed the edge of the glass. AJ felt the cold rise up, freezing the inside of her nostrils as she breathed it in.

A figure formed in the water. At first, it was a small green blob. It slowly took shape as it floated up from the depths of the bowl, up to the surface of the water.

A four-leaf clover. AJ sensed that it was the same one that Gladys had found just before her death.

Though there weren't any words, AJ had the impression that she needed to pick it up. She scooped her fingers into the ice-cold water. It felt thick and viscous, as if it was already partially frozen. When she drew her hand up, an actual four-leaf clover remained in the palm of her hand.

Thank you.

AJ just nodded, amazed at the leaf that was there, really there, in her palm.

Goodbye.

The familiar presence vanished.

AJ shivered.

What had just happened? How had Gladys managed that feat?

And was she now gone for good?

The weeks passed quickly. May arrived, summer and the full tourist season on the brink of starting. AJ was still only working part-days at the inn while still building up her psychic business. She was busier than ever, as the inn was one of the businesses in town sponsoring a BBQ tournament out at Sandy Point, headed up by Sandy, the woman in charge of Sandy's grill.

It was a glorious Wednesday, not too hot. AJ had had a nice swim in the ocean that afternoon and was just sitting down to lunch when a knock came at her door.

She wasn't expecting any clients so soon. No, the first wouldn't arrive for more than an hour or so.

Maybe it was a tourist who'd been walking along the beach and decided to see if the psychic was in, though AJ's neon-purple PSYCHIC! sign in the window was turned off and she had another sign that said CLOSED on the door.

People still stopped by anyway, sometimes.

She opened the door to a short Hispanic looking woman. She couldn't have been much more than five foot tall, with her long black hair worn in a thick braid hanging down her back. Her dark eyes held mirth, her thick lips were quirked up in a smile. She had curves and wore them proudly, her shirt a colorful red and gray, with black leggings. AJ estimated that she was in her twenties.

"Hello," the strange woman said. "I'm Gabriella."

She raised her hand, though not to offer it to AJ. Instead, she kept it between them, palm up.

A tiny blue flame appeared cupped in her palm.

"Carla sent me. She said you needed a teacher."

THE END

Kickstarter Bonus: Tarot Card Reading!

I did a series of simple three-card spreads. The first card is the past, the second card is the present, and the third card is the future.

I used a traditional Rider-Waite deck. I've had this deck since I was twelve years old. I've had (and used) other decks, but when I downsized to go live in a tiny house, I got rid of all the other decks and just kept this one.

The Wikipedia page lists all the images in this deck.

One of the things that I find is that every tarot card deck produces different sorts of results. The Rider-Waite deck is a good, general deck. I had another deck that was best for artist sorts of questions, yet another that mostly produced thin readings—it was difficult to get a deep reading from it.

I've developed my own relationship with this deck and the cards. There are symbols on the cards that speak to me, yet aren't necessarily mentioned in the literature or how to books. So my readings are personal, my deck and my reactions.

In addition, all three of the cards influence one another. Sometimes the meaning is pretty clear from each card as I go along. Other times, it isn't until the third card that the pattern makes sense.

FIRST READING

First card: Three of staves, reversed. You have a rich young man standing with his back to the audience, looking out over a cliff's edge toward the sea and the boat below. Three staves are planted around him, and he's slightly leaning on one of them.

This is a card about business, about enterprise, about new ventures. However, I drew this card reversed, so instead of the start of a business, it's about the end of one. I won't know more details until the end.

Second card: The Devil, upright. This is a major arcana card, number fifteen. The devil sits on a chair behind two humans who are chained to it, each of whom have tails and horns. This card is not reversed. It signifies failing effort to me, or a false outcome. Perhaps the business referred to in the first card has come to an end, or needs to come to an end, because the fruits of the business are no longer in line with the owner's expectations.

Third card: Four of pentacles, upright. Again, a business and prosperity card. The young man bears a crown and is very assured of his possessions, his arms wrapped around one of the pentacles.

This tells me that whatever business venture that is coming to an end in the first card will still proper. I believe that the devil card in the middle is an indication of change needed for the business to continue. That there's a choice there, and if the owner of the business makes the right choice, that there is prosperity in their future.

SECOND READING

First card: Page of staves, reversed. There is a fair young man standing in a desolate place, looking up at the top of the staff he holds in his hands. The staff is still blooming. The page wears a tunic covered in salamanders.

This page is a messenger, carrying news or announcements. As it's reversed, the news may be unsettling, and cause instability when it's received. It isn't evil news, and the page isn't malicious. But the news is important.

Second card: Six of staves, reversed. A young man proudly rides a light horse, carrying a staff with a wreath hanging from it, with five other staves in the background.

More news coming. Since this card is reversed, it isn't that the news is bad, just that there's a delay. The outcome of the news is uncertain.

Third card: Three of pentacles, upright. A sculptor is working in a monastery, showing his work to a couple of patrons. It involves craftsmanship, patronage, receiving rewards for hard work.

In this spread, I think that the news that's coming, that's mentioned in cards one and two, involves the work at hand. Though the work has been done, whatever reward is expected from this work is delayed. The news about the work will be large, but it will be slow in coming.

THIRD READING

First card: Five of swords, upright. A young man holds three sword, with an additional two at his feet. He looks over his shoulder with a smug expression at two figures in the distance, walking away.

Right now, I believe this indicates some sort of battle in the past. While the querant may have won the battle, the cost was also high, whether in terms of physical or psychological toll. Swords are always the card of rebirth, so it could be the start of a new venture that began wrong.

Second card: Ten of staves, reversed. A young man carries a bundle of ten staves over his shoulder. The burden appears heavy as he walks to town.

This indicates toil, burdens, success but at a cost. As the card is reversed, the struggle is intensified, and the rewards are less certain.

Third card: Page of swords, upright. A lithe young man swiftly walking across a rugged landscape, the winds blowing sharply. He is alert, on the watch for enemies.

In terms of the other cards, it seems to indicate that the journey is not over yet. Whatever was started in the past is still a burden, and the querant must remain vigilant in their dealings with this matter. The issue started rocky, requires a lot of work still, and that work won't be ending anytime soon. There is no indication as to whether or not this venture will be success or unsuccessful, just that it's going to continue to be difficult.

Sign up for my newsletter and I'll start you on your travels with a free copy of my book, *The Island Sampler*.

http://www.LeahCutter.com/newsletter/

Leah Cutter writes page-turning fiction in exotic locations, such as a magical New Orleans, the ancient Orient, Hungary, the Oregon coast, rural Kentucky, Seattle, Minneapolis, and many others.

She writes literary, fantasy, mystery, science fiction, and horror fiction. Her short fiction has been published in magazines like *Alfred Hitchcock's Mystery Magazine* and *Talebones*, anthologies like Fiction River, and on the web. Her long fiction has been published both by New York publishers as well as small presses.

Find Leah's books on Knotted Road Press at (www.-KnottedRoadPress.com)

Follow her blog at www.LeahCutter.com.

Reviews

It's true. Reviews help me sell more books. If you've enjoyed this story, please consider leaving a review of it on your favorite site.

Come someplace new...

Are you a traveler? Do you enjoy exploring strange new worlds, new cultures, new people?

Journey into the various lands envisioned by Leah Cutter.

Sign up for my newsletter and I'll start you on your travels with a free copy of my book, *The Island Sampler*.

I will never spam you or use your email for nefarious purposes. You can also unsubscribe at any time.

http://www.LeahCutter.com/newsletter/

About Knotted Road Press

Knotted Road Press publishes dynamic fiction set in exotic locations and unique non-fiction voices in genres such as autobiography, business, cookbooks, and how-to. Our authors cover a wide range of genres including science fiction, fantasy, mystery, literary, and poetry, appealing to all readers. We offer both DRM-free ebooks and print books for a global readership.

Knotted Road Press
www.KnottedRoadPress.com
www.KnottedRoadPress.com/Shop